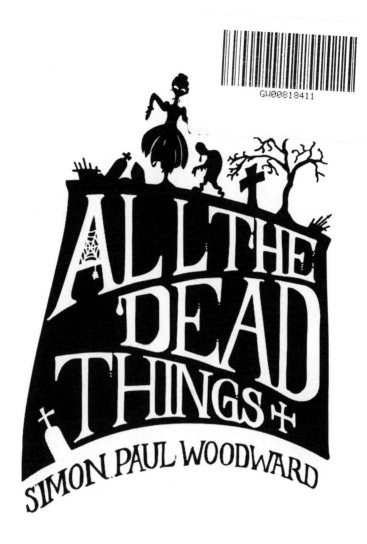

# ALL THE DEAD THINGS

## SIMON PAUL WOODWARD

First published in Great Britain, the US and Europe by
musingMonster Books, London in 2013.

Text copyright © Simon Paul Woodward
Illustrations copyright © Ellen Woodward
musingMonster logo © Neil Woodward

ISBN 978-1494366360


www.simonpaulwoodward.com
www.musingmonsterbooks.com

For my wife Tracy, who watches over
me while I'm chasing monsters

It starts in a supermarket.

The boy is three years old and trying to wriggle free of a shopping trolley's seat. His mum pushes him back down.

*Sit still.*

The boy ignores her, laughing as his dad walks away with exaggerated strides and flapping arms. The chicken walk; the boy loves his dad's chicken walk.

*Hurry up. Just get the eggs!* says his mum, smiling.

*Okay. Take a chill pill.* His dad winks as he turns into the next aisle.

His mum stacks tins into the trolley. She rubs her temples and scratches her arm. Cereal packets, a loaf of bread and bags of crisps follow the tins. She stops and the boy goes *umph!* as his chest bumps against the metal handle.

*Mummy. Naughty!*

She ignores him. Stares at her arm.

The boy is close to her. He can see goosebumps and golden hairs standing proud. Just like when his dad rubs a balloon against his jumper then holds above his arm saying: *look, magic*! His mum isn't smiling. She looks up, head flicking left and right.

*No, no, no.* She's muttering to herself.

The boy frowns.

*Mummy?*

She smiles at him, but there's something wrong with her smile. She steps away from the boy and peers around the end of the aisle, glances back at him and then moves out of sight.

He sees it.

The *monster*.

Human shaped, but grey-skinned with withered limbs and an emaciated body. Rotten clothes hang from its scarecrow frame. Its eyes are the colour of blood.

It's following an old man. His trolley has a wonky wheel that keeps locking. The old man curses with wheezy breaths, pushing his big belly against the handle as the trolley grates and judders. His face flushes with frustration. There's a curl of spittle on his chin. Sweat on his face. His lips look blue.

The monster circles the old man, facing down the aisle towards the boy, but their eyes don't meet. The monster's gaze is still fixed on the old man, who is now rubbing his hand in a circular motion on the left side of his chest, above his heart.

The monster shuffles to the left and … it freezes. It twitches, blinking rapidly, and slowly moves its gaze back to the boy. If the monster had eyebrows, it would have raised them. Instead, its bald forehead wrinkles and pus oozes from beneath a scab. It moves back to the right. The boy tracks it with his gaze. It moves left. The boy's eyes never leave it. A look of manic glee

5

creases the monster's face. It sniffs the air, then smiles, revealing half a dozen broken teeth in black gums. It claps its hands like a child waiting to be handed a present.

*It's you,* hisses the monster, edging forwards. *He was telling the truth. You can SEE me.*

It laughs and drops to all fours, scuttling towards Stan like a beetle.

*Mum!*

She's there in a second, skidding around the corner.

*What?*

*'onster!*

*What?*

*'onster!*

*Where?*

He points at the creature now hurtling towards them. She scans the aisle. All she can see is the old man. She grabs the trolley and wrenches it through a semicircle as the monster launches itself at the boy.

His dad is whistling and tossing a carton of eggs between his hands as he emerges into the aisle. He freezes when he sees the fear on the boy's face.

The monster can't change course, it's in midair. It smashes into the man, driving him into a tower of sweet corn tins. They crash to the floor; man and monster. Yellow tins roll in every direction. Somebody screams. Staff amble towards the incident.

The monster lands on his dad's chest and rolls off. His dad clutches his shirt above his heart, his fist scrunching fabric into a ball. Pain contorts his face. His teeth grind. His eyeballs are as white as a snooker cue ball.

The monster glances back and forth between the man and the boy, his expression pure frustration. He reaches out to the man and suddenly his hands are holding a ball of light.

The boy's rising into the air, twisting around. He can't see what's happening. His mum has pulled him from the trolley, clutched him tight to her chest and they're running. Running the wrong way. Running away.

*Daddy!*

They bustle past protesting staff and burst into a warehouse. The woman skids to a halt, dodging a forklift truck, then weaves between thirty-feet high pallets of shrink-wrapped boxes and tins.

*Which way? Which Way?* His mum panics at a junction.

*Daddy!*

She ignores him. She picks a direction and speeds up as they come to a huge doorway covered by heavy strips of plastic. Beyond is the blurred outline of the high street. They push through and sunlight blazes all around them.

*They've found us. Oh dear God, they've found us,* his mum says, as they run down the pavement. She flags down a bus and they jump aboard. Her hands are shaking. She spills coins on the floor as she pays. As they pull away the boy tugs at his mum's sleeve. She's looking backwards, out the rear window.

*Daddy?*

*I'm sorry,* she says, then; *What did you see. Back there?*

*'onster.*

Her lips pinch to nothing. The bus turns a corner and accelerates in a cloud of fumes. She sits back in her seat, squeezes him tight and closes her eyes. Tears roll down her cheeks.

*I saw an 'onster, mummy.*

# PART ONE

# MONSTERS

# 1

Somebody was ringing the doorbell. Stan woke with a start, pushing himself up from his tangled quilt on one arm. He cracked open an eye and peered at his clock: 08:30 TUES 12th APR. The doorbell rang again, this time a longer, sustained jangle.

"Stan, get out of your pit and answer the door." It was his mum, Lucy, calling up from their yard. He could hear the click of pegs and the rusty squeak of the clothes dryer as she hung out washing. The smell of her early morning cigarette hung in the air. She muttered the word *teenagers* just loud enough for him to hear.

*Only just,* he thought. His thirteenth birthday had been last week. Thirteen - old enough to make decisions.

The doorbell rang again, this time the short sharp bursts of a song: *why are we waiting.* Stan smiled.

"Stan! Get up and answer the door. You're going to be late for the ... for your appointment."

*His appointment.* He nodded. He'd go to his appointment, but it'd be the last time. Today, he was taking back control of his life.

He climbed out of bed, pulled on shorts and his favourite *Vampires Suck*! T-shirt and jogged downstairs to the front door shared by both the upstairs and downstairs flats. He smiled again when he saw the blurred, head-and-shoulders outline of a short figure with big hair through the frosted glass.

There was a newspaper sticking out of the letter box. The headline read: *INDIAN MUDSLIDE HORROR!* He wrestled it from the rusty jaws, tossed it in front of Mrs Cumberbatch's flat, and opened the door.

"Eventually," said Kalina, her iPhone held up in front of her face.

Beyond Kalina, on the opposite side of the road, Mr Williams was cleaning his windows and Mrs Williams was telling him how to do it properly, the bin men were emptying dustbins, a cat crept along the base of a bush towards an unsuspecting bird and cream coloured blossom drifted down landing on the head of a grey-skinned monster that nobody but Stan could see.

He blinked and averted his gaze, keeping the monster at the edge of his vision until it moved out of sight.

"You're doing that blinking thing," said Kalina continuing to film. "Stop it, you're ruining my shot."

"It's Tuesday," he said, the last syllable stretching out into a yawn. "I have to see my *you know what*."

"Your mental doctor, I know. You see your mental doctor every Tuesday."

"I'm not mental."

"Then why do you see a mental doctor?"

Stan would have punched any other kid in school (or any of the many schools he'd been to) for saying this, but with Kalina, he found himself laughing. She always spoke her mind, whether she was speaking to other kids or adults. Some people found her infuriating and rude, but Stan found her blunt honesty refreshing.

"She's a child psychologist. She treating my childhood trauma," he said.

"Hmmmm. Don't worry, you're not the only mad person in the world. My uncle Zgniweich married an ash tree ... or was it an elm ... anyway, I don't care, as we say in Poland - *Even a clock that does not work is right twice a day*. Nice shiner by the way. One of the Collins brothers?"

Stan touched the swollen pad of skin below his right eye. An image flashed into his mind: twisted expressions on the faces of his tormentors. A mob of kids at their back. Carl Collins pushing his tongue behind his bottom lip, making *uhhhh ... uhhhh* sounds. James Collins sings: *Psycho Stan, Psycho Stan, Psycho Stan!* Fists flying.

Stan held up two fingers.

"Two Collins brothers. Impressive," said Kalina. "What happened?"

"Nothing."

"Nothing looks considerably more dangerous than it used to be."

Stan shrugged, glanced over his shoulder and lowered his voice. "Anyway, what're you doing here? You're meant to come around later, when she's out."

"I know, but I was on my way to the park, to film some stock footage, and the perfect name for our film popped into my head. I had to tell you."

"Title number thirty-seven?"

"Don't be cynical."

"Go on then."

"Zoological Zombie Zone," said Kalina, lowering the phone and dragging a hand through gelled, purple hair that looked like an alien bramble bush. "Zed, zed, zed. I can see the logo already. Opinion, oh wise one?"

Stan grimaced.

"Not feeling the love?"

He shook his head. "Zombie animals? Absence of?"

"Ach! Details."

A door clicked open at the top of the stairs. Stan's mum stood on the landing glaring down at them. Kalina quickly hid the phone behind her back.

"Dzien dobry, Mrs W."

"Good morning, Kalina," said Lucy sucking on her cigarette and blowing a plume of smoke into the air. She shifted her attention to Stan. "If you don't get a move on you're going to be late for Jean."

"I'm going now."

"It looks like you're talking to Kalina to me. Listen, I've got an appointment at the estate agents so remember your keys."

Stan glared at this mum.

"Something to say?" she said.

They'd argued about moving flats again last night. She was thinking about moving to the other side of the city. He'd have to change schools. He'd lose contact with Kalina. He wasn't going to let it happen.

"Nothing," he said.

"Good. I don't want you posting any more films on the internet. Do I make myself clear?"

"But everybody ..."

"You're not everybody. Have I made myself one-hundred percent clear, Stan Wisdom?"

Stan grunted a *yes*.

"Promise me," she said pointing her cigarette at him.

"Mum!"

She raised her eyebrows.

"I promise."

"Good. Now get a move on and stay out of trouble. And make sure you don't lead him into any, Kalina." Lucy turned and disappeared back into the flat. Stan pulled a face at the space she'd occupied.

*

Stan and Kalina walked down the street towards the park. Many of the houses had been split into flats and most were in need of love and attention. They passed a parade of peeling window frames, high weeds and gap-toothed fences.

"What's your mum's problem with the internet? She one of those people who think computers give you brain cancer?" said Kalina.

"She's worried about weirdoes and stalkers." Stan shook his head. "You name it, she worries about it."

"Does she think they are going to reach out the screen and grab you?"

He shrugged.

"They prey on weaklings with no brains and no friends. You, Stan Wisdom, definitely have at least medium brains and you have at least one friend - me. I, of course, have more brains and at least one friend - you. Therefore, I conclude we are safe from all the weirdostalkers out there and we should continue with our masterpiece in secret. Agreed?"

Stan felt a tightness in his chest when he glanced at Kalina. It was true, she was his friend. She had a runaway mouth and the strangest sense of style (today: big purple hair, three layers of ripped T-shirts, a short tartan skirt, neon-pink tights and Doctor Martin boots) but she was his friend and that was something he'd never had before.

Throughout his thirteen years, he and his mum had moved flats at least eight times. He'd never had time to settle in any school and make friends. He was always the outsider, the new kid arriving with a reputation for fighting, and every schoolyard gang-lord and nut-case was drawn to him like iron filings to a magnet. Stan didn't want to fight. He didn't want to be sitting in a head teacher's office listening to the same lecture with his mum sniffing back tears and promising he'd change, but he had no choice. The other kids would find out about his weekly *appointment*, the name calling and whispers would start, and the bullies would find him an even more irresistible target. If he didn't fight, he'd just be the new kid with a dark secret that everybody laughed at and picked on. He'd be a nobody at the bottom of a pile of nobodies and he wasn't going to live like that.

It was the *appointment* that was the problem. Lose the *appointment* and he'd lose the target on his back.

Today, he was going to lose the *appointment*.

Kalina had befriended him on day one at his latest school. He was sitting outside the head teacher's office sporting a fat lip and swollen cheek after his latest playground welcome. She was waiting to be disciplined, for the *tenth* time she proudly told him, for wearing a non-regulation uniform; if you could call an outfit of a leotard, blue-spotted wellies, tutu and Peruvian poncho a uniform.

"Are you the new boy with the bad attitude?" she said looking straight at him from beneath dark, frowning eyebrows and an explosion of pink hair.

"I didn't start it."

"Hmm," she said, tilting her head as she studied his face. "Want to be in my film? There's a character who's been badly beaten up in it. I'm the queen of special effects, but make-up costs money."

"Film?"

Kalina slipped an iPhone from her pocket and showed him a clip. She was being chased, screaming down a corridor by a shambling zombie with strips of skin uncurling from its cheeks.

"Cool."

A day later, he shot his first scene. A week after that, she announced that he was going to be co-director and co-producer on her unnamed zombie masterpiece that they'd shoot for pennies on an iPhone and sell to Hollywood for millions.

More important than any of this to Stan - he had a friend.

"Oi, oi psycho Stan, where d'you think you're going?"

Stan snapped out of his memories. Two kids his age were sitting on a dilapidated car's bonnet a couple of gardens ahead of them. One had a crusted cut on his top lip, the other a black eye mirroring Stan's. It was Carl and James, the two youngest Collin's brothers, he had fought the day before.

"Psycho! Psycho! Psycho!" chanted Carl, wrapping his arms around his body as if he was wearing a straight jacket.

"Don't say anything," said Stan, taking Kalina's hand.

He'd fought them yesterday and won. He'd fought them last week and won.

"I said: where you going?"

Stan ignored them. He was sick of their battles. He knew that only silence could prevent another fight. Once you engaged with a bully, once you looked them in the eyes and traded insults, the situation would escalate, ratcheting up the tension to a point where violence was the only possible outcome. He dragged Kalina forward. The bonnet *dinged* as the Collins brothers jumped down.

"Oi! Gypo Girl! Don't they have manners where you're from? We speak to people in the street. This isn't gypo Polandski," said Carl. James cackled.

Stan sensed Kalina starting to turn. He speeded up, marching her forward. "Ignore them."

The t-junction at the end of the road, and the park beyond, was ten metres away. If they made it there without getting drawn into a fight, they might be able to lose them in the woods.

"Psycho, why does your mum wears wigs? She a psycho?" said Carl.

"Yeah, what's it like having a psycho for a mum?" They were both cackling now.

"His Dad was probably a psycho too."

*His Dad was probably* ... Hot rage enveloped Stan. If they wanted another fight, he'd give them one. His hands curled into fists and his lips pulled back from his teeth. He spun around to face Carl and James, but found himself facing all four of the Collins clan. The two younger boys, and their huge, sixteen-year old twin brothers, Fran and Daz.

"Something to say, Psycho?" said Daz, smiling. "Before I kick your head in."

"Ready when you are," said Stan, shifting his weight onto the balls of his feet. The Collins brothers spread out in front of him.

"Stan?"

It was Kalina. He'd forgotten her in his swirling rage. He glanced at her and then back at the Collins brothers. They were here for revenge. To crush his one boy rebellion against their neighbourhood tyranny. They wanted to hurt him and it was likely Kalina would be drawn into the fight.

"Run," he yelled and they pelted towards the t-junction.

Kalina held her phone above her head.

"What ...?" said Stan.

"Footage," she said, as they jumped down the curb and sprinted across the road towards the green wall of trees that marked the edge of the park.

They didn't see the white van with *CLEAN ME* scrawled into the dirt on its side until it was too late. The driver swerved right, screaming curses and slamming his hand against the horn. Stan threw himself into the gutter, feeling air suck him backwards. Blossom petals and dust danced in swirling patterns as he jumped to his feet.

"Come on," he said dragging Kalina into the woods.

Across the road, the Collins brothers had gathered around James, who'd twisted his ankle avoiding the van.

Daz looked over his shoulder. "Don't worry, we know where to find you, Psycho."

## 2

Stan and Kalina sprinted into the park and plunged into the woods. When they were sure they weren't being followed, they split up, agreeing to meet later at Enzo's cafe.

"Why the serious face?" Kalina had asked as they parted.

"Stuff to sort out."

"I hate stuff. It's overrated."

"Me too."

Dragging his feet, Stan climbed the little hill at the centre of the park. On three sides, trees heavy with white blossom stretched to the edge of the park, only interrupted by crisscross pathways and black patches where kids had lit fires. If arson ever became an Olympic sport, Stan was sure this neighbourhood would produce a medalist. The final side was given over to football pitches.

He caught a glimpse of Kalina's purple hair. She was heading for an exit as far away from the Collins brothers as possible.

He sat cross-legged and pulled his dad's lighter from his pocket. It was a Zippo with a flip-top and an enamel knight wielding a sword and shield on its side. He flicked it into life and watched the flame bob and weave.

"Hi dad. Really need your help today."

The flame bent in a gentle breeze.

"I've worked out what to do. How to make things better. I need to stop seeing the counsellor - Jean. Wherever we go, whatever school, the kids always find out. A kid seeing a counsellor, every week; got to be a psycho, weirdo, nutcase hasn't he. Soon as they find out I'm a walking target."

He took a deep breath. Swallowed the knot of fear rising into his chest.

"The only reason mum makes me see Jean is the monsters. It's a waste of time. The monsters are real. They aren't going away, whatever the counsellor says. They killed you. I've seen them kill other people too."

The lighter was getting hot. He extinguished the flame and sucked his thumb.

Ever since the monster killed his dad in the supermarket, he'd seen them. It wasn't every day, but never more than a few days passed without him seeing one. There were many types, all vaguely human shaped, but each was grey-skinned, red eyed and twisted by a unique grotesquerie. Over the years he'd started using names for the different types: *tree monsters, mangled monsters, smokey monsters ...*

He flicked the lighter back to life.

"This is the last time I see Jean, Dad. The monsters are real, but I can hide from them. I've been doing it all my life. It's the bullies I can't hide from. They find me, I fight them, I get suspended, mum gets upset and we move schools again. Well, now there's Kalina and ... well, I'm not ... I've had enough."

He extinguished the flame and slipped the lighter into his pocket. It felt warm against his thigh.

"I've got a plan."

\*

Jean's consulting room was in an alternative therapy practice in a large Victorian house that had been painted pastel pink. *The Johnson-Patel Clinic* read its sign above a montage of smiling faces. Wherever he and his mum moved to in the city, and they had moved often, Stan always saw Jean. For the first time, he was living in a flat close enough to walk to her practice.

In the distance black clouds rose like a tsunami wave and thunder rumbled. He shivered and hurried inside, waving to the receptionist as he headed for Jean's room.

"Hi Stan," she said, showing him to the usual big leather chair.

Jean was a very tall, thin woman and today she was wearing a stripy dress that made her look like a stick of seaside rock. She sat down, crossed her long, booted legs, slipped on her rectangular glasses, scanned a page in her notebook and smiled at Stan. Outside, thunder rumbled again.

"So, how's your week been? What happened to your ..." She waggled a finger around her eye.

"Walked into a door," said Stan.

"Hmmmmm," said Jean, and the session started just as every other session had for the past few years.

Jean would ask him what he'd been doing at school, at home and with his friends. She'd scribble notes, making reassuring humming noises and nodding wisely as he answered. These gentle interrogations normally lasted ten minutes. After that, she'd shift her position in the chair, lean forward earnestly and ask about the *visitors*. Stan was never allowed to call them monsters. Jean said the word itself was part of the problem.

The first time Stan had seen a monster was the day they murdered his dad. When he told his mum what he'd seen, she'd become angry and tearful, telling him to stop talking such nonsense. Then she'd hugged him and apologised and cried some more. Later she told him his dad had suffered a heart attack. Stan shook his head and said no, it was the monster.

A few days later he saw another monster. Stan was walking down the street with his mum and there it was, sitting cross-legged on a car staring at a busy junction. Just like the other monster, it was grey skinned and wearing tatty clothes, although they were of a style Stan had never seen before. The monster only had half a face and one arm. Its single eye swivelled as it watching passing cars. Stan didn't let on he could see the monster. He remembered what had happened to his dad.

After that, he saw monsters regularly and grew increasingly afraid that he'd wake to find one perched on his chest, a twisted arm reaching out to choke him. When he told his mum he was seeing more monsters, he saw her face change; a light left her eyes and her muscles sagged. She seemed to age years in seconds. He didn't know what this meant but it scared him. She hugged him, telling him repeatedly that the monsters were just something

23

in his mind. He had to ignore them. It was after this his mum arranged for him to see Jean and they had started to move flats every few months.

He'd seen monsters kill on two more occasions. Once, he and his mum had been on a bus edging past a car crash. Firefighters were trying to cut free the driver of one car, but Stan knew they were too late. He could see a monster, all twisted limbs and cuts, leaning over to steal a ball of light from the man. The second time, old Mrs Saunders, who was living across the road from them at the time, had been wheeled from her house on a stretcher by paramedics. Unseen by anybody but Stan, a monster had been riding the stretcher too, perched on all fours over Mrs Saunders. Neighbours said Mrs Saunders died of natural causes on the way to hospital.

"Penny for your thoughts," said Jean.

He'd drifted away."Sorry."

"So, how have the *visitors* been this week?"

*Deep breath, determined face, it's now or never.*

"I haven't seen any. They're gone."

Jean's pen hovered over the pad. Her eyes, swollen by her glasses lenses, flicked up.

"None?"

"None."

"Well, that *is* progress isn't it?"

Stan smiled.

"Has something changed. Something that might be helping you?"

Stan ran through his lines in his head. He'd been working on them for a month now, trying to find the courage for this day.

"I thought about what you said in the last session, about *really* trying to fight this and … well … I did. I saw a visitor and I said the words you taught me: *you're not there, you're not there.* I just repeated them over and over. I did it for a few days and ..." he opened his arms wide. "They were gone. You were right."

"I see." Jean scribbled notes.

*I'm doing it. I'm really doing it!*

"When did you last see a visitor?"

Stan paused, pretending to think. He blew out his cheeks. "Last Thursday, I think."

"So you haven't seen a visitor for five days?"

"Brilliant isn't it?"

Scribble, scribble. Jean put down her pen and looked up, eyes as large as eggs. "Are you are telling me the truth, Stan?"

"Of course I am." Stan winced at the weakness of his voice. He could feel his cheeks colouring. "I ... yes."

Jean stared at him. Not in a harsh, intimidating way, but with intelligent compassion. Stan's cheeks were burning. The silence stretched out. It seemed like minutes since either of them had spoken. Stan willed himself to keep his mouth shut. He knew what she was doing; trying to force him to fill the silence with a confession.

"Honestly," he said. "Scouts honour."

"I didn't know you'd joined the scouts."

"I haven't. No ... but ..." He was searching for words to convince her when he knew he should really just keep his mouth closed.

How could this be happening? He'd played out the scenario so many times in his head. Pictured himself leaving the clinic for the last time with Jean wishing him well for the rest of his life. Pictured the rumour sweeping through school ... *have you heard? Stan isn't seeing the madness doctor anymore. He isn't a psycho!*

"Stan, you wouldn't be the first person to try to escape a difficult process by pretending everything was okay when it wasn't. I'll ask you again. Are you really being honest with me, and, what is more important, with yourself?"

"Yes."

"Stan?"

Silence again. The rapid beat of his heart. Rising anger. The clock ticking. Jean raised an eyebrow.

He couldn't stop the words erupting. "It's not fair!"

"Stan, it's ..."

"This is pointless. The monsters are *real*. I know they are, I've seen what they can do."

"Stan ..."

"I could see you a thousand times and it wouldn't do any good. They're never going to go away, but I can handle them. I know how to make sure they think I'm just like anybody else. I know how to stay safe. But ... but ... as long as I come here, I'll be the mental kid. I don't want that anymore. I've got a friend now. I want to *belong* somewhere."

He took a deep breath. He was almost panting after his tirade.

"Is there anything else you want to share?" said Jean. His outburst hadn't ruffled a single professional feather.

"I'm never coming back here."

There was no going back now. If he couldn't dupe Jean with his story, he'd have to take control himself.

"I don't think that would be a good idea, Stan."

"I do."

*Scribble, scribble, scribble.*

"I'm going," said Stan, standing.

"Please don't. Just stay a few more minutes. Help me to understand your thoughts."

Stan was rooted to the spot, trapped between his anger and Jean's implacable professionalism.

"Please," she said, patting a hand on the chair.

With a grunt of frustration, Stan plonked himself back onto the cushion.

"What's brought all this on?" said Jean.

"Everything. This isn't helping. I don't want to move again."

"You're worried about losing your friend ... Katlina?"

"Kalina." Stan sighed. "Yes, and other things. She isn't my girlfriend, if that's what you think. We make films together."

"What sort of films?"

When the word left his lips he knew he'd made a fatal error. "Horror."

*Scribble, scribble, scribble.*

"I think we'll have to have a discussion about that. That sort of thing might not be helping with the visitors."

"They're nothing to do with this," said Stan, standing. "I know what I'm doing. I'm not coming back."

"Stan, you're a junior and you can't stop attending these sessions without parental permission. If you want to stop, I'll have to speak to your mum. I'll have to tell her you weren't entirely honest with me today and have a discussion about the films."

He'd lost. He was trapped. He opened his mouth but no words came out. Red faced, he banged out of the room, slamming the door behind him. As he burst out of the clinic, thunder ripped across the sky, setting off a car alarm. His thoughts were in such turmoil he barely noticed it.

Jean was going to call his mum.

It wasn't fair. For the first time in his life he had somebody who understood him and who he could trust and all his mum and Jean wanted to do was stop him seeing her. He wasn't going to let it happen.

Blind to his surroundings, he bumped into pedestrians, pushed past them, snarling with frustration. A man called out after him, but Stan didn't hear him. His mind was churning; white noise for thoughts. His chest was tight. He was struggling to breathe. Everything and everybody was conspiring against him.

Ahead of him was a t-junction. Sitting on a wall staring at the junction was a monster. It wasn't a *visitor*; it was a *monster* with grey skin and crushed limbs. It looked like it had been dragged beneath a lorry. Heart pounding, Stan crossed the road. He kept the monster in his peripheral vision, maintaining the illusion of invisibility, just as he had all his life. As he got closer, he could see it's face was a pulpy mass of cuts and bruises. A chunk of skull was missing revealing glistening brain tissue. Blood filled eyes peered out of the mess.

Monsters had ruined his life. They'd killed his dad, made him live every day in fear and driven him to Jean's clinic and all the bullying that that brought down on his head. He hated them with an intensity he couldn't articulate.

He didn't know he was going to speak until the words left his lips. "Leave me alone!" he yelled directly into the monster's face.

With a yelp, the monster fell backwards off the wall and whacked it's head on the floor. It leapt onto all fours, back arched, hissing at him.

"I said: leave me alone!" Anger chased away Stan's fear.

Hissing again, the monster backed away from him. It extended a bent arm.

"Seer," it said, blood bubbling on it's lips.

Then twisting, it leapt up onto the wall and loped away down the street on all fours like a dog.

Stan was shaking. His breath coming in ragged gulps.

*He'd chased a monster away.*

All these years he'd pretended they weren't there, letting them do what they wanted, letting fear rule his life. All he needed to do was stand up to them. Just like any other bully.

He lent forward, planting his hands on his knees. "Bye bye monsters," he said, waving at the empty street.

# 3

"Meat ... fresh meeeeeaaat," said Stan, his head lolling from side to side. His face was mottled green and strips of skin hung from his cheeks exposing raw, weeping flesh. Outside, lightening flashed and thunder followed immediately, rattling the windows. Rain lashed against glass.

Stan looked down at his hand, flat against the table, fingers spread wide, and a grin split his face. He picked up a carving knife. He studied the blade, then satisfied it was sharp enough for the task, sliced off his index finger. Blood ran across the table. His finger rolled free, pink and lifeless. He picked it up and dangled it above his open mouth, groaning in anticipation.

"Time to feed," he said and lowered the finger to his lips.

"Carry on," said Kalina from behind her iPhone.

Stan stood still, the finger poised above his open mouth.

"Eat it!"

"I'm not going eat a raw sausage," said Stan dropping out of character and slapping the sausage onto the table.

"Why not?"

"Number one: Food poisoning. Number two: it's got one of your mum's false fingernail glued to the end."

Kalina grunted. "We all have to suffer for our art."

"I don't see you doing much suffering. I'm the one with streaky bacon glued to my face."

"You're the star. Think of all the fans you'll have."

"There's no point in having fans if you're going to be in hospital with food poisoning."

"Details. All details. Okay, we'll cut away just as you're about to put it into your mouth. You can chew on something else."

Lightning strobed again and a crack of thunder shook the house. Next door's dog started to howl.

Stan froze. "Did you hear the front door?"

They stood in silence, listening.

"Nothing," said Kalina. "I think we should stop filming now. I don't want your mum to catch us."

"It's okay. Things are going to be different now," he said, but there was no conviction in his words.

"You promised."

Stan plonked himself down on the sofa. "She won't be back for a while."

After he'd chased away the monster, Stan had met Kalina at Enzo's Cafe. He'd been high on his victory as they raced the storm back to his flat. Kalina set about transforming him into a zombie and as always, the brilliance of her make up amazed him.

His euphoric mood had soon started to darken. His mum would take Jean's call badly. He imagined her on the phone; nodding, apologising, her lips tight with rage, her cheeks flushing red. Cutting off the call. Stuffing the phone into her handbag as she thundered back to the flat, a human storm racing nature's creation.

Kalina sat by him on the sofa and started to review the scene they had just shot. "Is it true your mum wears wigs?"

"What?"

"Wigs. You know, like the Collins brothers said."

"Since when do you listen to what they say?"

"Just interested."

Stan pictured the scene. It was just after he'd started at the school. He'd been fighting and his mum had been called in to see the headmaster. He'd been sent home for the day. It was windy. As he and his mum left a branch snagged in her hair and yanked off her wig. The Collins brothers, faces pressed flat against the classroom window howled with laughter.

"Sometimes."

"Does she have cancer?"

"No! She just likes to change her hair style a lot."

Kalina grunted and scrubbed back through the scene. "I've also noticed that your mum often changes glasses."

"What' s wrong with that," he snapped, irritated by her questions. Questions that nagged at *him,* but he tried to ignore.

"Just unusual," said Kalina, as always apparently immune to his mood changes. "It's none of my business, but is she running away from somebody?"

"No, of course not. How come you think you know so much about my mum."

"As we say in Poland: *A guest sees more in an hour than the host in a year.*"

"As we say in England: Mind your own bloody business, big nose." He rubbed his forehead. A headache had crept up on him out of nowhere. It must be the heavy storm air.

"I don't have a big nose," said Kalina checking her reflection on the iPhone screen.

"My mum's all I've got."

"You've got me too," she said, then grunted and pointed at the screen. "But you won't unless you start practicing your zombie shuffle."

"What do you mean?" said Stan leaning over her.

"You look like an old woman waddling to the bog."

"No way," said Stan.

Neither of them heard the downstairs door open or footsteps climbing the stairs. Thunder hid the sound of a key turning in front door. Suddenly his mum was standing in front of them, her wig soaked through and clinging to cheeks flushed red with anger.

"You promised," she said.

"We're just looking at an old film," said Stan.

"With bacon stuck to your face?"

"I'd better go," said Kalina.

"I think that's a very good idea, young lady."

"It's not Kalina's fault."

"I know whose fault it is. You lied to me."

Kalina slipped her iPhone into her pocket and with a nod to Stan, left the flat.

Lucy slammed her keys onto the table. Stan's headache clawed at his brain.

"You looked me in the eye and promised me," she said.

"It's harmless."

"It's not harmless." She threw a handful of sodden leaflets onto the dining table. "I've just had a conversation with Jean. She tells me you're planning to stop your sessions."

"We're not moving again," he said pointing at the leaflets.

"We are and you're going to be seeing a new counsellor."

Stan grabbed the leaflets as his mum headed into he kitchen.

"Scotland! *Scotland!* No way. I'll never see Kalina."

"You'll make new friends," she called out.

He followed her into the kitchen. She was stuffing a key with an ornate *L* shaped fob into a little wooden box on the window sill. She looked flustered as she pushed it back into the corner.

"No, I won't. Kalina's the only friend I've ever had. Ever."

"That doesn't mean you won't make another."

"Scotland. You've got to be bloody joking."

"Don't you dare swear at me, young man." She pointed at him, hand shaking.

"Dad wouldn't have wanted to live in Scotland."

"Dad isn't here."

"I wish he was. I wish he was here instead of you." Stan wanted to pull the words back as soon as they were out his mouth. Lucy's eyes filled with tears.

"Tough, you're stuck with me."

"It's not fair."

"Life isn't fair. The sooner you learn that the better."

"Why do we have to move?"

"We just do."

"Are you running away from someone?"

Lucy turned and stared at him. "What? Why did you say something stupid like that?"

"I'm not stupid."

"Then stop acting stupid."

Stan rubbed his head. The headache was burrowing into his brain, spreading tentacles of pain. He flapped the leaflets. "All this. Moving. Moving again."

"The landlord put the rent up."

"So we have to move all the way to Scotland?"

Lucy sighed and wiped away tears. "It's time for a change. *I* need a change. A rest."

"What about me?"

"You'll grow to like it."

"I won't. This is home. Kalina's my friend. I don't want to live somewhere they eat deep-fried Mars Bars."

"You don't understand how things work."

"No, I don't. I don't understand why you do weird stuff like wearing wigs and changing your glasses everyday? Why you won't let me post stuff on the web? Why you're so paranoid."

Lucy's eyes filled with tears again. "So I'm a weirdo now, am I? That's a nice thing to say to your mum."

"I don't want to move!"

He knew his words were hurting her, but he couldn't stop himself. His headache was throbbing, lights darting in front of his eyes. He'd chased away a monster today. He didn't need Jean. This was supposed to be a good day. Why did his mum have to destroy it?

"Nor do I," shouted Lucy, throwing her arms up in the air. "You can't always do want you want in life can you?"

"You can, I can't," said Stan, stomping out the room and slamming his bedroom door behind him.

He threw himself down on the bed and clutched a pillow to his face. Waves of pain jagged through his head. Soon he heard sobbing and smelt cigarettes. The loft ladder grated and squeaked as his mum wrestled it down. Suitcases rang against the rungs. He'd lost. They were moving.

Stan wasn't sure how long he'd been lying there, teeth gritted against the headache, head beneath the pillow, when the knock came on the bedroom door. It squeaked open and footsteps crossed the room. The mattress creaked as his mum sat beside him.

"I'm sorry, Stan. I didn't mean to shout at you. It's been a bad day."

"I'm sorry too," mumbled Stan from beneath the pillow.

"Take that off your face," she said gently prying his hands free and pulling away the pillow.

He screwed up his face and rubbed his forehead.

"What's the matter?"

"Bad headache. Flashing lights and everything."

"That's a migraine."

She fetched painkillers from the bathroom and he swallowed them.

They sat in silence for a while. Lucy pursed her lips and took a deep breath. "I know we don't have the most normal life.

We've probably moved flats more times than some people have had hot dinners."

Her smile was weak as she collected her thoughts. Then she spoke, her voice quiet and fragile. "There are real reasons for what I do. Serious reasons. Complicated reasons. I've kept them to myself until now because it isn't right to burden a child with them. You're growing up so quickly now. Look at you, you're like a little man." She stroked his cheek.

Stan was finding it difficult to breathe. His mum had never talked to him in such serious, adult tones before. He could feel the weight of her words as if they were stones pressing on his chest.

"It's time for me to share some things with you now. It'll help you understand. It'll make things easier."

"I'd like that," said Stan, screwing up his eyes as another wave of pain stabbed into his brain.

"Pills not helping yet?"

"Worse."

Lucy sighed. "Then this isn't the time for a serious conversation like this."

"Yes, it is," said Stan pushing himself up and then slumping back onto the bed, groaning and clutching his forehead.

"Tomorrow," said Lucy. "We'll talk tomorrow. Now lie still, close your eyes and let the pills do their work. Call if you need anything."

"But ..."

"No buts, close your eyes."

He closed his eyes. The bed springs pinged as she stood up. She walked across the room. The door handle squeaked.

"Mum?"

"Yes, Stan?"

"I chased one of the monsters away today."

"That's good," she said, but Stan heard a catch in her voice.

His bedroom door clicked closed and his mum tiptoed across laminate flooring. Her lighter clicked and hissed to life as she lit another cigarette.

*It's time for me to share some things with you now. It'll help you understand. It'll make things easier for you.*

What things?

Stan dozed fitfully, his headache curdling into bad dreams. Time lurched by in disjointed chunks; monsters in the park, monsters in his bedroom. He rolled around in bed, sweat making the sheets sticky as flypaper. His migraine was getting worse, mixing with the sound of great machines throbbing and churning as if they were in the room with him. In his delirious state he knew they were just part of a dream. What else could they be?

He woke with a start. It was dark. He was still half in and half out of the dream. The pain was almost unbearable. Hot wires in his brain. Pressure against his skull like the jaws of a vice. He tried to call out to his mum, but his mouth was parched and his cries emerged as strangled whispers. He flopped out an arm, reaching for something to throw to attract her attention, but his fingers clutched fresh air. Pain sawed into his forehead. His eyes bulged.

He rolled over onto his side. He was face to face with his bedside clock. The time was 23:59. The engine noises screamed to an even greater pitch. He gritted his teeth. Dug the heels of his palms into his forehead. His skull was breaking apart into a jigsaw of grinding bone.

*I'm going to die*. The thought was a cold certainty.

The clock ticked over to 00:00 and somewhere in the fraction of time between the change of days, in the space between a tick and a tock, the deafening noise, all the pressure and pain, vanished. Stan pulled his hands away from his head, still tense, waiting for the next wave of pain, but it didn't come. He took a deep shuddering breath and closed his eyes, squeezing tears of relief onto his cheeks.

Sleep took him like a shark snatching a seal into the deep.

# 4

Somebody was ringing the doorbell. Stan woke with a start from a dreamless sleep and pushed himself up from his tangled quilt. He cracked open an eye and reached for the glass of water on his bedside table. It wasn't there. His mum must have taken it away. He touched his forehead and sighed with relief; no migraine. The door bell rang again.

"Stan, get out of your pit and answer the door." It was his mum. He could hear the rusty squeak of the clothes dryer as she hung out washing. The smell of her early morning cigarette hung in the air. She muttered the word *teenagers* just loud enough for him to hear and Stan shuddered: *déjà vu.*

The doorbell rang again, this time short sharp bursts ... *why are we waiting* ...

"Stan! Get up and answer the door. You're going to be late for the ... for your appointment."

"What?" he muttered clambering from his bed. Had his mum booked him in to see Jean again as punishment for yesterday?

He sighed when he saw Kalina through the front door's frosted glass and hesitated, hand on the door knob. This wasn't wise. His mum would go ballistic if she saw her. He pulled the newspaper from the letterbox and tossed it in front of Mrs Cumberbatch's door.

"Eventually," said Kalina as he opened the door. She had the same gelled-up, purple hair and was holding her phone in front of her face.

Beyond her, on the opposite side of the road, Mr Williams was standing on tip toes cleaning his windows and Mrs Williams was telling him how to do it properly; the bin men dragged wobbly dustbins across the pavement; a cat crept along the base of a bush towards an unsuspecting bird; pink and cream blossom drifted downwards, landing on the pavement.

Stan shuddered again as another wave of déjà vu washed over him.

"Stop twitching. You're ruining my shot."

"You shouldn't be here," said Stan glancing over his shoulder.

"Why?"

"Yesterday."

"What about yesterday?"

"Did they ban memory in Poland or something?"

Kalina lowered her phone. "What're you talking about, Stan Wisdom?"

"Bacon glued to my face. Parental rage. Ring any bells?"

Kalina muttered something in Polish and then said: "I think you've been having bad dreams. Look, I was on the way to the park to film some stock footage and I thought of the perfect name for our film. I had to tell you."

"I hope it's better than Zoological Zombie Zone," he said.

Kalina's mouth dropped open. "Are you telepathic?"

"What? Why? No."

41

Kalina hummed spooky music and raised her eyebrows. "That's freaky."

"That was your idea yesterday."

"I just came up with it today. Just now," said Kalina, pointing over her shoulder.

Stan laughed. "Is it April Fools Day?"

"No, it's Tuesday 12th. I'm not winding you up."

"It's the 13th," said Stan.

"12th."

"13th!"

Kalina held out her arm. She was wearing her favourite retro LED watch she'd bought from a charity shop. Stan always joked that it looked she was wearing a toaster on her wrist. She pressed a button and the time changed to the date: 12:04:13.

"You changed it before you got here."

"Stan, really, what is your problem? Today is Tuesday 12th April." Kalina pointed at Mrs Cumberbatch's door. "Check the newspaper."

Stan grabbed the newspaper: INDIAN MUDSLIDE HORROR, shouted the headline. His eyes raced to the top of the page. TUESDAY 12th APRIL.

Stan looked back at Kalina: three layers of ripped T-shirts, a short tartan skirt, neon-pink tights and Doctor Martin boots. "You're wearing the same clothes."

"Have you bumped your head?"

The landing door clicked open. Lucy glared down at them through a cloud of cigarette smoke. Kalina quickly hid her phone behind her back.

"Dzien dobry Mrs W," she said.

"Good morning Kalina," said Lucy blowing more smoke into the air. She looked at Stan. "If you don't get a move on you're going to be late for your appointment."

Stan looked at Kalina and then back to his mum. There was no way that they would have collaborated on a joke at his expense. They were barely on speaking terms.

"That was yesterday," he said.

Lucy sighed. "Is that meant to be some pathetic attempt to wheedle out of seeing Jean?"

"But ... wait here," said Stan running upstairs into his bedroom. He grabbed his bedside clock: 08:34 TUES 12th APR.

The room tilted around him. How could this be true? Had he dreamt an entire day? Had his victory over the monster been nothing but night wishes? The storm, the argument with his mum, his migraine; none of it real?

He walked past his mum and back down the stairs to Kalina.

"Have you caught up with the rest of the planet now?" said his mum.

Stan nodded. He didn't know what else to say or do.

"Good. Listen, I have to go out later so remember your keys. And I do not want you posting any more films on the internet. Do I make myself clear?" said Lucy.

Stan nodded.

"Good. Now get a move on and stay out of trouble. And make sure you don't lead him into any, Kalina." Lucy turned and disappeared back into the flat.

*I dreamt those words. I dreamt all this. How can I have dreamt all of this?*

He left the house, striding along beside Kalina, but feeling as if he was on one of the moving pavements that carried people around airports. A moving pavement to whisk him through his dream day.

"What's your mum's problem with the internet? Is she one of those people who think computers give you brain cancer?" said Kalina.

Stan shrugged. "She's worried about weirdoes," he muttered, thinking, I know what's coming next. *Does she think they ...*

"Does she think they are going to reach out the screen and grab you?"

Stan shrugged.

"They only prey on weaklings with no brains and no friends. You, Stan Wisdom, definitely have medium brains and you have at least one friend - me. I, of course, have more brains and at least one friend - you. Therefore I conclude we are safe from all the internet crazies out there and we should continue with our masterpiece in secret. Agreed?"

Stan didn't reply. He was lost in his thoughts: *Please don't let the Collins brothers be there.*

"Oi, oi psycho Stan, where d'you think you're going?" said James.

"Psycho! Psycho! Psycho!..." Carl wrapped himself in his arms.

Stan grabbed Kalina's hand and dragged her forwards. He didn't want to play out the whole charade. Not now he knew what was coming; the racism, the taunts about his mum and dad, the older Collins brothers.

He heard the bonnet *ding* as the kids jumped clear.

"Oi! Gypo girl. Don't they have manners where you're from? We speak to people in the street. This isn't gypo Polandski."

Footsteps followed them down the street. The t-junction. He had to reach the t-junction. If he could escape his street maybe he could shake free of this madness.

"Psycho, why does your mum wears wigs? She a psycho?" said one and the other laughed.

"Yeah, what's it like having a psycho for a mum?"

"His Dad was probably a psycho too."

This time he didn't turn around. He knew that Fran and Daz Collins were standing shoulder to shoulder with their younger siblings.

"Run," he yelled, and they sprinted towards the t-junction.

Kalina raised her phone, filming the pursuit, then arms windmilling for balance, they leapt from the curb and sprinted towards the park.

Stan only remembered the van with *CLEAN ME* scrawled into the dirt on its side when its horn screamed like a trapped animal. He rolled across the gritty pavement amidst a tornado of blossom and dust. He was on his hands and knees, then Kalina was beside him, saying something, pulling him to his feet and leading him into the park.

Stan didn't hear Daz's yelled curses, or pay attention to Kalina's attempt to drag him deeper into the woods. He just stood still, staring at the unbelievable scene before him.

# 5

The woods were full of monsters. There must have been at least forty in his eyesight and it took all his will power to divert his gaze into his practiced *seeing but not seeing* peripheral vision. They sat in groups of three or four, all grey skinned, with their twisted limbs and tatty clothes, chatting in animated tones. Some, themselves as thin as branches, perched amongst the foliage calling out to each other with voices that rustled like autumn leaves stirred by the wind.

A bloated monster with heavily-veined skin, wearing a decomposing leather jerkin, and a patch over one eye, passed Stan and spoke to another group of monsters.

"'Ello gents. Any idea what this is all about?" Water splashed from his mouth as he spoke.

"Whisper is, it's good news about the big man," said a female monster. Her bloodshot eyes peered out from a face burnt and cracked like spilled Tarmac.

"Good news? More lies you mean." More water fell with his words.

"Watch what you're saying. Moses has ears everywhere," said the burnt monster glancing around.

"Understood. Obliged to you." The bloated monster bowed and stumbled onwards.

The whispered words were out of Stan's mouth before he could stop himself. "Can you see them?"

"They're still on the other side of the road," said Kalina, looking over her shoulder.

"Not them," whispered Stan keeping his gaze locked forward.

"Huh?"

"Can you see anything in front of you?"

Kalina turned to face him and spoke deliberately, as if to a very young child. "They are called *trees*."

Stan felt breathless. He'd never seen so many monsters before and a wild optimism had flared inside him; maybe something had changed, maybe somebody else would be able to see them too. Nothing had changed. They remained *his* monsters. He was alone with them.

"I've got to go. I'll be late for my appointment," he said in a quiet voice.

"Okay. Want to shoot some scenes later?"

Stan shook his head.

"You okay?"

"Tomorrow. Tomorrow I'll be okay," he said walking away.

He tried to count the monsters, grey blurs in his peripheral vision, but by the time he had crossed the park, he'd given up. There were hundreds. Some were no more than bundles of stick-thin bones and wispy hair, fragile enough to be moved around by the wind. Others moved awkwardly on twisted limbs like broken clockwork toys. He saw more of the bloated monsters dribbling water as they talked. Burnt monsters and others covered with terrible wounds. Headless monsters and others with milky eyes and chattering teeth.

He let out a long, shuddering breath as he exited the park. His face ached from the false calm he'd plastered on it. As he arrived at *The Johnson-Patel Clinic*, black clouds filled the sky just as they had in his dream. Thunder rumbled. The air was thick and heavy.

"Hi Stan," said Jean, showing him to the usual big leather chair. Of course, she was wearing the stripy dress that made her look like a stick of seaside rock. She sat down, crossed her long, booted legs, slipped on her rectangular glasses, scanned a page in her notebook and smiled at Stan. Every action just as in his dream. Outside, thunder rumbled closer.

*I can't have dreamed all this. Every detail. That just ... doesn't ... happen.*

"So, how's your week been? What happened to your ..." she wiggled her finger, and so it began.

Stan wanted the appointment to be over as quickly as he could. It wasn't a real appointment, it was a dream, or the day that followed a dream of the day before or ... whatever, he needed time to think, to try to work out what was happening to him.

He forced a happy expression onto his face, choking down his anxiety and focused on giving Jean the answers she wanted to hear:

"Yes, I've seen a couple of *visitors* this week."

48

"I did exactly what you said: ignored them and repeated: *you're not there, you're not there.*"

"My mum says I've been much better this week."

He didn't think he'd fooled Jean with his easy answers. She smiled quizzically as she drew the appointment to a conclusion.

"I'm glad things have improved, Stan. Remember, you have my number if you need to talk before our next appointment. Okay?"

Stan nodded, smiled and left as quickly as he could. As he walked out onto the street, a massive clap of thunder set off a squawking car alarm. He bumped into a man and carried on down the street without apologising. The man called out after him but Stan didn't hear him.

Ahead of him was the t-junction where the monster had been sitting. This time the wall was empty. *Everything is the same except me and the monsters*, he thought.

People and houses were a blur as he slowly wandered through the city. He wasn't taking the most direct route, but he had no doubt where this winding path would lead. He was being drawn back to the park; back to the monsters.

*This can't be happening,* he thought. *Ignore them. Turn around. One foot in front of another. Go home. Shut the curtains. Go to sleep. Wake up and it'll be tomorrow.*

He didn't go home. By the time his wanderings delivered him to the park the storm was overhead. Lightning flashed edging trees with sudden silver. The heavens boomed beneath a thunder hammer.

Stan entered the park. The monsters were still there, even more numerous than before; thin monsters, fat monsters, tall, short, dismembered and disfigured, all with their dead grey skin. *Why had they gathered here?* He had to know. Choking back his fear he thrust his hands into his pockets, and moved quickly, trying to look like a normal boy racing home ahead of the storm.

Fat rain drops pattered against leaves and pockmarked the dusty paths. Stan picked up his pace. In seconds, the rainfall became a downpour, soaking him and slicking his hair to his scalp. He blinked through a stream of water and shivered. The monsters sat huddled in their small groups chatting.

Blinking away raindrops, Stan saw a group of a dozen or so monsters approaching, moving from group to group with an air of importance. Stan gazed past them, eyes fixed on a distant point as they grew larger in his peripheral vision.

The lead monster was a towering figure, well over six feet tall. He had a mop of red hair and a big bushy moustache that joined up with equally bushy sideburns. Amidst all the hair, Stan could see patches of grey skin and blood filled eyes. The monster wore a faded, red military tunic with gold buttons, black trousers with a red stripe down the side and heavy boots. The ornately carved hilts of three daggers stuck out of the left side of his chest above his heart. The red tunic was stained an even deeper red around them. He carried himself with a presidential air, chin high, red eyes glittering.

Alongside him was one of the stick-thin monsters wearing green robes. White hair fell to his shoulders and beneath harsh red eyes, his wrinkled cheeks were covered with swirling tattoos.

Surrounding these two was a ring of a dozen hulking monsters acting as body guards. All had been disfigured by violence. One had an axe protruding from the back of his head, another a gaping, bloody hole at the centre of his chest as if a cannonball had passed straight through him. All these monsters sported armbands bearing a three dagger emblem.

As they came closer, Stan heard the monster soldier speaking.

"Yes, brothers and sisters. Tomorrow, when we are all gathered, then I will be able to share great news with you," he said, slapping backs and squeezing shoulders. "You'll see the true leader I am. See what I've been doing for you all these years. You'll all be there for me won't you. None of you is going to let me down now is you?"

He stroked the knives in his chest and the monsters muttered *of course not, no, we'd never let you down, Sergeant Moses.*

Stan's heart lurched as the monster strode towards him through the rain. Lightning flashed and caught on the silver dagger hilts. Had he given himself away? Had he stared for too long? Desperately he fixed his gaze on a distant tree.

"Humans," said the monster stepping in front of Stan and then keeping pace with him but walking backwards, his blood filled eyes fixed on Stan's face. "If only they knew what we did for 'em. Oblivious they is. Oblivious of the universe's mysteries. Rushing around like ants what's thinking their business has any meaning when all they're doing is lifting leaves."

*You're not there! You're not there!* Stan forced himself to keep his focus away from the monster, not to stare into those bloody eyeballs.

Sergeant Moses danced a jig in front of Stan, hopping from foot to foot, sticking out a black tongue. He laughed, the sound rattling and wet, as if his lungs were full of blood. "Don't worry little ant, we're here to save you when the time comes."

He stepped off the path, out of Stan's way, and beckoned the other monsters to him with an impatient wave. "More work to be done, boys. The word needs spreading like butter on burns." He laughed his wet laugh again.

Stan released a ragged breath. His body was shaking. Turning a corner he sprinted along the path through the park, the driving rain and thunder. He dared a glance back. Was that the monster with tattooed cheeks watching him from a copse of trees? He snatched up a thick branch with a sharp point a couple of feet long and held it like a sword. *Please don't let them know I can see them.* He dived into the woods and a shortcut home.

"Wait," said a monster stepping out from behind a tree, thrusting out his arms, palms open.

Fear coursed through Stan as his momentum carried him towards the monster.

*He knows I can see him!*

The monster had the shape of a young boy, shorter than Stan. Grey skin. Blood filled eyes. His left cheek caved in like a windfall apple. He wore tatty old fashioned clothes, the sort of rags urchins wore in the Charles Dickens film Stan's English teacher had shown the class. His arms were oddly bent, as if they each had an extra elbow. His chest was flat and spread wide, straining against its dirty shirt. A half-coin charm hung around his neck.

"Please wait!" said the monster.

Stan reacted instinctively, lashing out with the branch. He had time to see the monster's bloodshot eyes widen with horror, then brilliant white light detonated in his head and icy pain immobilised his arms.

"Mercy," whispered the boy monster.

Suddenly ...

*... you are somewhere else: a busy street lined with tall, grand buildings. Men wearing long, black coats and top hats, walking sticks clicking against the pavements. Women with bonnets and wide skirts. It is dark. Gas lamps hiss and cast puddles of buttery light. Horse drawn carriages clatter over wet cobblestones splashing you.*

*"Out of the way wretch!" snarls a man with bushy sideburns slashing at you with his walking stick.*

*You feel the polished wood sting your skin. You lose your footing and fall backwards, stumbling into the road. A girl screams. Fingers grasp your sleeve but your momentum carries you into the road. Into the path of a carriage and it's iron-shod wheels. Onto your back, the wheels crunching over cobblestones and ...*

... Stan was back in the woods, reeling on the spot, feeling nauseous. What had just happened? He'd stabbed the monster with the branch and now it was gone. There was a cool sensation on his fingertips. It was the monster's half-coin pendant. He ran, shaking his fingers, trying to lose the pendant, but its chain tangled around his fingers and he stuffed it into a pocket.

When he got home, his hands were shaking so badly it took him a minute to fit his key into the lock. He had to hold his right hand with his left hand and grit his teeth. What had he done? What had he seen?

He stumbled up stairs; into the flat, into the kitchen. His mum, dripping wet, was hiding the key with the *L* shaped key fob in the little box.

"Stan, what's happened?" said his mum taking one look at her son and pulling him to her.

Stan blinked back tears and caught his breath. On the table behind her he could see estate agent leaflets showing flats in Scotland.

"Stan? Tell me. What's happened? You're shaking like a leaf."

"Some kids. Never seen them before. Not from my school." A lie was always going to be easier than the truth.

"What did they do?"

"Nothing. They couldn't catch me."

"You're sure they haven't touched you?" She passed him a towel. "Dry your hair."

He nodded and stepped away from his mum's embrace, breathing more calmly. He pointed at the table. He had to know what she'd say. Had to know if the day was still repeating itself. Had to know if the madness was going to get madder.

"We're not moving again?"

"When you can afford to pay the rent you can choose where you want to live," said Lucy. Her voice was calmer than yesterday, but the words were the same.

"These flats are in Scotland. I'll never see Kalina again."

"You'll make new friends."

"No, I won't. Kalina's the first proper friend I've ever had. It's not fair." Stan said the words without passion, as if reading a dull play at school.

"Life isn't fair, Stan."

Stan shook his head. He didn't have the appetite for any more repetition and he didn't want to fight with his mum. He touched his forehead. Another thing had changed from the day before; he didn't have a migraine.

"Mum, now that I'm getting older, are there any secrets you want to tell me?"

"What? Where did that question come from?"

"We're always moving house and stuff like that."

"That's just landlord problems. Rents and deposits and things like that. Nothing for you to worry about."

Stan clearly remembered her words from the day before: *There are real reasons for what I do. Serious reasons. Complicated reasons. I've kept them to myself until now because it isn't right to burden a child with them. You're growing up so quickly now.*

She'd said these words after they'd argued and he was lying ill in bed. After she'd sat alone smoking and thinking. His behaviour had changed the dream, or repeated day or whatever it was. He wasn't going to get her to reveal secrets just by asking. For a second, he contemplated starting an argument, feigning a migraine, running back to his room and slamming the door, but he couldn't be sure if this would work. He needed time to think.

"I'm going to read in my room for a bit," he said.

"Get out of those wet clothes first."

He shut his bedroom door and peered out the bedroom window. Lightning flashed and thunder rumbled. More monsters were walking down the street in the rain. One peered up towards his bedroom window and Stan ducked down beneath the sill.

What was happening to him? What was happening to the world?

That night he read a book by torchlight under his quilt to stay awake. When he heard his mum turn off the television and smoke a final cigarette, he switched off the torch and pretended to be asleep. She always looked in on him before she went to bed. He checked his bedside clock: 22:00. He waited half an hour. Surely she would be asleep by now. He tiptoed into the kitchen and made as strong a cup of coffee as he could stomach.

Steam rose around his face as he sipped the strong brew. He peered through a crack in the curtains at the dark streets. A monster without legs drifted through a pool of neon light then disappeared into the dark again.

If he could stay up all night; if he was awake when one day became the next, maybe he could find out what was happening.

Eleven o'clock passed and tiredness tugged at his eyes. He stood up and walked around the room.

At eleven fifteen he ate a slice of toast slathered with jam. At eleven forty-five he made another cup of coffee. His eyeballs felt gritty and raw. Eleven fifty. Eleven fifty-five.

"I won't fall asleep," he muttered as he circled the living room.

He opened his eyes.

He was opening his bedroom door, a yawn splitting his face. He couldn't remember leaving the living room. He slapped himself on the face and went back to the living room. *I won't* ...

This time he woke as he was climbing into bed.

"No." The word morphed into a yawn.

He struggled back across the bedroom. Every step felt like he was slogging through mud. He yawned again. His thoughts were slow, thick and foggy. Why was he fighting this? Sleep would be *so* good. He reached out for the door handle, but he wasn't there yet. Where was it? His head had drooped forwards, weighty as lead. He wrenched it up and the door receded as if the bedroom were made of chewing gum and somebody was pulling it away from the clenched teeth of reality.

Stan stumbled forward, arm flailing, hand grasping, yawns consuming him and ....

# 6

The doorbell rang and Stan woke with a start.

*No ... no ... no ... no.*

He grabbed his alarm clock: 08:30 TUES 12th APR.

*This cannot be happening!*

He rubbed his eyes and looked at it again; the time and date didn't change. Yesterday hadn't been a dream. Today was the same day as ... as what? Yesterday? The day before?

The door bell rang again. His mum called up from the garden. Stan pulled on his clothes and thundered down stairs, yanking the newspaper from the letter box and opening the door; purple-haired Kalina filming him.

"I've cracked the name for the film," said Stan, before she could speak.

Kalina carried on filming. "Hmmm. Me too. You first."

"Zoological Zombie Zone."

Kalina lowered the phone and her mouth dropped open. "No way! That's *exactly* what I just thought of."

"Great minds and all that," said Stan, starting to close the door. "Look sorry, I've got to run and I won't be able to do any filming today. I have stuff to do for my mum, okay."

"Oh, okay," said Kalina, taken aback. "Is everything all right?"

"Yeah. Sure. See you tomorrow. Same time, same place," said Stan and shut the door.

His mum appeared at the top of the stairs.

"I know. My appointment. I haven't forgotten," said Stan before she could speak.

Lucy opened her mouth but Stan jumped in again as he ran back upstairs. "I'll take my keys in case you're out later."

He grabbed a Darren Shan novel and ran back downstairs. Outside, he turned right, running up to the main road, and then back down the next parallel road, avoiding the Collins brothers.

The woods were just as he'd left them; full of monsters. Now they were in motion, a wave of grey bodies moving through the trees towards the far side of the park. Summoning a relaxed expression, Stan wandered amongst them, alert for Sergeant Moses and the tattooed monster. He climbed the little hill at the centre of the park, sat crossed-legged and opened his book.

In front of the hill, the large field was covered by thousands of monsters. More were streaming onto it from all sides. They crowded together in a tight mass, finding space where they could, pushing and shoving. Fights broke out as space became harder to find.

Stan snapped his attention back to his book as a dozen muttering monsters walked past him over the brow of the hill and jogged down the other side towards the gathering.

"Do you think it's true?"

"All talk ... All talk..."

"If it exists, we kill it. It's the only way."

"It *don't* exist. It's all part of his story."

"Watch out his armbands are everywhere."

When Stan peeked over the book again, the crowd were facing a low mound on the far side of the field. All except for a semicircle of hulking monsters, each wearing an armband with the three-dagger insignia, who faced the crowd, roughly pushing back any who came too close.

A red-jacketed figure climbed onto the mound. Sunlight glinted on the daggers embedded in his chest. It was Sergeant Moses. The green robed monster with tattooed cheeks stood behind him. He ran his bloodshot gaze over the crowd, then looked up towards the hill. Stan lowered his gaze, feeling the hairs on his arms and the back of his neck bristling.

*Keep calm, Stan. He can't see you watching him from there.*

Stan glanced up. The tattooed monster had returned his gaze to the crowd. Sergeant Moses raised his hand. When the muttering continued, he leant forward and yelled.

"Silence!"

He let the murmurs subside.

"Why are we here? I'm sure that's what you is wondering. Why have I summoned each and every one of you from around the world? Why have I pulled you away from your important work?"

He paused.

"Believe me, it is not something I would do unless it was of the greatest importance. This *is* of the greatest importance. Today I'm going to share a great secret with you."

The tide of murmurs rose and fell.

"As our beloved leader, Death, was slipping into a coma, thirteen long years ago, he passed a secret on to me. He knew that only I, his true friend and his right hand, could be trusted with it."

*Death? He'd said their leader was Death?*

"A secret so powerful it could destroy us all. He knew we'd need a strong leader to meet the danger. It was then that he named me his heir. He begged me to take all his powers, to declare myself the new Death, but I, loyal servant that I am, said no. I would not abandon hope that my friend would recover. I would only take his powers temporarily, to help fight this threat and I would return them when our enemy was defeated."

A commotion broke out in the middle of the crowd, monsters pushing and shoving, fists and voices were raised. A space cleared with a lone monster at its centre.

"Liar!" shouted the skinny monster, as smoke poured from his mouth. "You did it! You used magic on him! You put him in the coma!"

Monsters wearing armbands barrelled through the crowd pushing aside any who stood in their way as they cut a path towards him.

"Down with Moses! Long live the Resistance!" screamed the monster, his head consumed by a cloud of smoke. The armbands smashed into him and dragged him, still protesting, into a copse of trees. There was a scream, then silence.

Sergeant Moses shook his head sadly. "Our great leader's illness is a terrible thing. It's hard to take, I know. It's sown confusion and fear. It's made some of you see conspiracy and wrong doing where it don't exist. It's turned us against each other.

Now is the time for that to end. Those who call themselves The Resistance. Who question my right to govern. Lay down your arms. I will forgive your treachery. I know there are more of your amongst this crowd. Raise your arms, step forward from the shadows and let me hear your grievances. If you don't, I'll take it as a sign you are all united with me."

Monsters turned to look at each other muttering. Some stood on tiptoes, craning their neck, peering across the crowd. Nobody raised an arm or spoke out.

Sergeant Moses smiled. "Good. We are united! It is safe for me to reveal the secret. The true cause of Death's terrible malady."

Absolute silence fell across the field. Even Stan was holding his breath.

"Before the coma took him, he told me a *monster* had been born to a human woman. A monster born to prey on our kind. This monster he named the Seer."

The word spread across the field; a wave of whispers ... *the Seer ... the Seer ... Seer ...* Goosebumps covered Stan's flesh.

"This monster feeds on our energy. None of you is safe. It's evil, powerful and most terrifying of all, it has the power to *see* you!"

There were gasps across the field as monsters repeated his words ... *see us ... it can see us!*

*No* thought Stan. *No, no, no.*

"Death said he could feel the Seer draining his power, like a leech sucking blood 'til it was fat and plump. He said, if it weren't destroyed, it would eventually be the doom of us all." Sergeant

Moses pointed at the crowd. "You, you and you. All of you, will fall into slow sickness as the Seer feeds on you, if it ain't destroyed."

"For thirteen years, I, and those close to me, have hunted for it in secret without success. We sought to protect you without sowing fear. But this creature's brood mother hid it well. It's grown stronger, feeding on our great leader. Now he clings to existence by a thread. Even I started to fear the Seer might never be found and Death might be lost. Not now. Oh no, not now! Yesterday, the Seer revealed his identity to us!"

The monsters cheered, some surging towards the stage where the armbands linked arms, holding them at bay.

*Oh please no.*

"Now we have the tools to find this creature and save you all. We have the tools to save Death. Kill the Seer and save Death! Are you with me!"

"Yes!"

"This is why I have summoned you here today. Every last one of you from around the world. Together we will hunt down this Seer!"

A bloodthirsty roar ripped across the field.

"While you hunt, you will not be able to save souls, so last night, I broke Time. This day, Tuesday 12th of April, will now repeat itself until I repair the break. Nobody will die while time is suspended unless we choose that they die. You can hunt for this creature knowing that innocent souls have not been put at risk. As the day ends, the people will fall into the deepest of sleeps and when they wake, they will repeat the same day. Not the Seer. He is special. He will stand out like an ugly thorn amongst sweet petals."

Armbands moved amongst the mass of monsters distributing leaflets.

"Now we know what the Seer looks like," said Sergeant Moses. "Now *we* can see *him* too. It's a fair fight and the hunt is on. We think its lair is close to this place. Grab a leaflet. Burn this creature's face into your mind and then go out and hunt it down. Are you with me?"

The monsters roared their approval. Sergeant Moses snatched a knife from his chest, holding it high so that sunlight glinted on the bloody blade.

"I said: are you with me?"

This time the roar was deafening. Monsters waved disfigured and twisted limbs in the air. They surged towards the armbands, grabbing the leaflets and passing fistfuls around. A monster with only two fingers spilled a bundle onto the ground and a gust of wind snatched them up and set them fluttering through the air with the blossom.

A sheet landed face down close to Stan. He knew what he was going to see on the paper before he picked it up. In an instant, he was up and running, heart thumping, as he sprinted down the hill away from the monsters.

Onto the flat grass and through the trees. He could still hear Sergeant Moses voice, the monsters roaring, baying for his blood. Clouds of fallen petals swirled around his feet. He sneezed and stumbled. He ran through branches and snagging undergrowth, then burst onto the pavement, launching himself out onto the road.

He didn't see the van with *Clean Me* scrawled in the dirt on its side until it was too late. Wide-eyed and shouting, the driver whacked his hand against the horn. The vehicle lurched forward as the brakes bit, acrid smoke streaming from the tyres. Long black skid marks scarred the tarmac.

Stan froze in front of the van. It was too late. He'd never get out of the way in time. He closed his eyes and it was on him. His hand released the sheet of paper and it was ripped though the air, landing face-up in the gutter. Above a badly drawn sketch of Stan's head and shoulders were the words:

## THE SEER

## WANTED DEAD OR ALIVE

# 7

Stan opened his eyes. He was still standing in the road. Parallel skid marks ran either side of him. *That wasn't possible. That wasn't ...*

"What the hell?" said the van driver, jumping out. He starred at the skid marks and Stan standing between them. He starred at his van and then back at Stan. He shook his head. "Ain't possible. This is a dream," he said.

*A nightmare,* thought Stan as the world spun around him and the road rose to smack him in the face.

\*

"You must have swerved to avoid him." A gentle Jamaican accent. Stan knew this voice.

"I know what I saw. I ain't saying it's makes no sense, but I was there. I was driving right at him. I dunno. I just, dunno." A man's voice. Rough and full of fear. "Guess I must have done."

"Look, he's going to be fine. If you have to go, please go. I won't say anything to the police." His mum's voice.

"The police? Do me a favour, love. Wasn't me running out into the road."

"How fast we're you driving? Vans have instruments for measuring that sort of thing don't they, so your employers can check up on you."

Stan's eyes flickered open. He could see three blurry figures.

"I didn't have to come knocking on doors to find where he lived did I?"

Stan's vision started to clear. He could see the van driver edging his way to the door. His mum glowering at him. Mrs Cumberbatch, from the downstairs flat, a supportive hand on his mum's arm.

"Let him go, Lucy," she said. "Let's look after Stan."

"See yourself out," said Lucy.

"Eh, you don't know where bloomin' Paradise Street is do ya. Me satnav's bust and I forgot me A to Z. I've been driving round for an hour."

"Never heard of it. Close the door on your way out," said Lucy.

Stan heard the lorry driver thump down stairs and slam the door.

"What happened?" said Stan. His voice was croaky.

"You tell me." Lucy had tears in her eyes. "Bloody stupid boy. You could have been killed. What have I told you about being careful."

"Lucy, it's okay, he's safe, no need to shout," said Mrs Cumberbatch.

"Don't tell me what to say to my boy," said Lucy, then instantly reached out to Mrs Cumberbatch and mouthed sorry.

"No need to apologise to me, darling. I know what it's like. I've three of my own. They're all in the thirties but they may as well be thirteen."

The image of the van, centimetres from his face, flashed into Stan's mind and stayed there like the ghost of the sun when you stare at it for too long.

"The van?" he said.

"Good job he was an experienced driver," said Lucy.

"Should be a racing car driver," said Mrs Cumberbatch.

"Not many people would have been able to swerve around you like that," said Lucy.

*Swerve around you? The van centimetres from his face. No room to turn. No time to swerve. I should be dead.*

"He didn't."

"Didn't what?" said Lucy.

"Swerve."

Mrs Cumberbatch laughed. "Then you must be in heaven looking upon two of the Lord's prettiest angels.

*Nobody will die while time is stopped unless we choose that they die.*

The downstairs door slammed open and they all jumped.

"What the ..." Lucy strode out into the hall and padded downstairs. Stan heard the front door slammed shut again. "He must have left it open," said Lucy coming back into the room.

"Go on, get up there and check it out. You got your poster?" The voice came from downstairs, loud and harsh. Stan knew the voice: Sergeant Moses. "I said: have you got your poster?"

"Yes!" a girl's voice. Soft steps climbed the stairs.

Stan looked back and forth between his Mum and Mrs Cumberbatch. Why couldn't they hear the voices? Why couldn't they hear the footsteps?

Lucy was reading the instructions on a box of pills Mrs Cumberbatch had given her. He heard the words *sleeping tablets*, *hyperactive*, *doctor* and *needs to sleep* but his mind wasn't joining the words into sentences.

A monster entered the room. It was shaped like a girl about Stan's age. She wore a scruffy, old fashioned dress, faded black and fringed with dirty lace. As always, her skin was grey. The girl moved into the room on limbs with too many joints, both arms jutting at odd angles. She rocked as she walked and looked at him with blood filled eyes.

*Don't look at her. Don't look at her. She's not there, she's not there...*

Stan's mantra was in vain. His eyes were drawn to the girl.

"Open wide." His mum was forcing open his mouth, popping a pill on to his tongue. She lifted a glass to his lips. "Swallow."

He swallowed, but kept his eyes on the monster.

"Well, is it him, we ain't got all day?" said Sergeant Moses.

The monster slipped between Lucy and Mrs Cumberbatch, unrolling her poster. Stan pushed himself back against his headboard and screwed up his fists. They wouldn't take him without a fight. He remembered the monster in the woods; the sudden flash of light, the out of body experience, the pendant.

"Stan, what's the matter?" said his mum.

Stan ignored her.

"Gabby! Damn you, is it him?" shouted Sergeant Moses as heavy feet thudded up the stairs. "I'm coming to check myself."

The monster held up the poster and looked back and forth between it and Stan. She nodded. Then smiled. Her teeth looked unnaturally bright in her grey face.

"No," she shouted. "This isn't the Seer."

The footsteps halted. "You sure."

"Sure as eggs's eggs."

"Well, get down here. Plenty more houses to check."

"Coming boss," said the monster called Gabby, then lent forward to whisper to Stan. "You have friends. Stay in this house and out of sight. This poster ain't great, but it's good enough for somebody with sharp eyes. Like me. I'll be back to move you soon as its safe."

Gabby turned, her body rocking and arms moving awkwardly as she made for the door.

"Why are you helping me?" said Stan.

"What did you say Stan?" asked his mum.

"It's just the pills starting to work," said Mrs Cumberbatch.

Gabby looked back at Stan.

"'Cause Moses is a liar. You aren't a threat to Death. You're Death's heir and the only hope we've got of saving him," she said and left the room.

# 8

Stan struggled to pull himself free of the bedclothes. A carousel of questions spinning in his head. His mum and Mrs Cumberbatch pinned him down cooing soothing words. His mum started to cry.

"He's traumatised, Lucy darling, the pills will calm him," said Mrs Cumberbatch.

She was a large woman and she used her weight skillfully to pin him to the bed. Within a couple of minutes, the pills took effect and he had a bowling ball for a head, blurred vision and limbs made of clouds. His eyes closed as he heard footsteps leave the room.

Later, he woke briefly and heard somebody moving around in the loft above his bedroom. *Big mice,* reasoned his befuddled mind. *Very big mice.* He struggled free of the pill's grip again just before midnight. He stared as his clock until it ticked over to 00:00. Just before sleep snatched him back into oblivion, he thought, *tomorrow will be different.*

It wasn't: The doorbell ringing. 08:30 TUES 12th APR on the alarm clock. His mum calling up from the yard. Kalina at the front door. Indian Mudslide Horror. Zoological Zombie Zone. *I'll see you later,* he tells Kalina. His mum says she's going out. *I'm not,* says Stan.

The day passed in a blur. Same songs on the radio. Same news on the television. Mr Williams cleaning his window. The white *Clean Me* van zipping down roads searching for Paradise Street.

*'Cause Moses is a liar. You aren't a threat to Death. You're his heir and the only hope we've got of saving him.*

Thunder rumbling. Lightning. The storm unleashed. His mum returning, dripping wet.

"You missed your appointment with Jean. You can't do that, Stan. Listen to me, you're ..."

He wasn't listening.

*You're his heir.*

The words spun through his head. They made no sense. Night came and sleep took him. He didn't dream. He woke with a clear head and a plan. When he'd made his excuses to Kalina and his mum had left, he started rooting around under the kitchen sink. He emerged with a battered packet of blond hair dye. Before his mum started wearing wigs, she'd often coloured it instead and he remembered the stink of ammonia that used to fill the flat. How he'd walk around with a peg on his nose making her laugh, back in the days when she still laughed.

By the time Stan had worked his way though the instructions (wet hair, comb through, leave for five minutes, rinse, repeat ...) the kitchen was swimming in water and he was blinking away stinging tears. He dried his hair and gelled it up into punky spikes, slipped on a pair of spiderman sunglasses and dressed in the brightest T-shirt and shorts he owned.

When he was very young, his Dad used to perform magic tricks for him. He'd move a coin from knuckle to knuckle, smooth as a caterpillar ripple, before it vanished into one hand.

"Which hand?" his dad would say, offering closed fists.

Stan would giggle, knowing that whichever one he chose it would be, magically, the wrong one. He'd tap the right hand: empty. The left hand: same outcome. Then his dad would twirl his hands and pluck the coin from the air beneath Stan's nose.

"Where's the best place to hide things, Stanley?" he'd say, and they'd repeat the answer together.

"*Under your nose!*"

Lifting his sunglasses, Stan admired his reflection in the mirror. Even Kalina would be impressed by how garish he looked.

"I'll be right under your nose, Sergeant Moses."

The streets were empty of monsters. Their hunt must have moved on to another part of the city. He jumped on a bus and headed for town. As rows of houses gave way to the retail parks fringing the city centre he saw them. Hundreds of them were already about their work, picking locks, climbing drainpipes, slipping through open windows. All of them clutched wanted posters.

"Gabby, where are you?" Stan scanned the street.

At the next stop, he left the bus. Thrusting his hands into his pockets, he took a deep breath and strode out amongst the monsters. Through the sunglasses' lens they looked like warped shadows.

The big department store at the heart of the city centre was launching another sale and its windows were covered with red posters shouting *75% OFF TODAY ONLY!!!* A large crowd had already gathered at the entrance waiting for it to open. People pushed and shoved to get closer to the front and a chance of a bargain, oblivious to the monsters moving around them, checking their faces against the wanted poster.

Stan forced himself to whistle when a one-armed monster wearing a wetsuit paused to check his face against the poster. The monster moved on. His disguise was working.

"Gabby."

She was on the other side of the road, her rocking walk carrying her into a shopping arcade. He dodged between cars, restraining the urge to call out to her. He couldn't risk drawing the attention of other monsters.

The shopping arcade had a carved ceiling and was home to antique shops and the city's most famous bookshop. Gabby stopped to look at a display for a book called *The Hourglass World* in the window. She was alone.

"Gabby!" The word came out halfway between a whisper and a shout.

She turned around. The monster had no bottom jaw and her black tongue lolled down onto her neck. She pointed at Stan and screamed, her tongue flapping like a flag in the wind.

Stan froze, speared to the spot by the ululating wail. The monster started towards him, still pointing, speeding up. Slapping footsteps sounded at the far end of the arcade. More monsters on the way. Stan broke free of the spell, turning and fleeing into the street.

Monsters were sprinting towards the scream from every direction, unsure who to chase, but sensing that their prey was close. The jawless monster ran out of the arcade, still screaming and pointed at Stan. A hundred pairs of eyes fell on him and the monsters charged. He spun on the spot. The street was blocked in both directions. Tall buildings hemmed him in. No way out. On the monsters came, red eyes, grey skin, twisted limbs, water and smoke and wounds; two walls of broken bodies ready to crush him.

At the edge of his vision he saw red. He sprinted across the road towards it and the monsters bent their run in pursuit. Without breaking his stride, Stan leapt forward, skidding across a car bonnet and threw himself into the crowd slowly funnelling into the just-opened department store.

"Oi! There's a queue here you know!"

"Watch your elbows!"

"There's enough bargains for everyone, innit!"

Stan ignored curses and dirty looks as he pressed deeper into the mass of people, spreading waves of agitation with his progress. He glanced over his shoulder. He was in the centre of the crowd. There were at least ten rows of people between him and the pursuing monsters, who were milling around behind the crowd in confusion.

A security guard opened a second door to relieve the congestion and the crowd protecting his back started to peel away. Monsters surged into the space.

"There's 95% off in the sport department! I've just seen it on Twitter," he shouted, holding up his hand as if cradling a phone. "95% off all trainers!"

A shockwave of excitement ran through the crowd as the shopping sharks smelled blood. It quickly rose to yells of excitement as Chinese whispers mutated the *95% off* into *99% off everything!* A group of teenage boys started pushing forwards and others followed. Girls screamed and pushed back. The crowd surged forwards, refilling the gaps behind Stan and carrying him into the store.

As he cleared the doors, Stan dodged through the frenzied shoppers, some already scooping up piles of clothes, towards the kids department. He hid behind a pillar and glanced back to the entrance. Monsters were pouring in after the humans. He bent low, hiding behind clothes displays as he made his way deeper into the store. He pulled off his sunglasses and stuffed them into a bin. He grabbed a baseball cap, a pair of jeans and a white shirt and dared a glance above the clothes racks; there were monsters everywhere. He also saw the sign he was looking for: Changing Rooms.

Keeping low, he headed for the sign. When he passed the edge of the eyewear department he grabbed a pair of reading glasses from a shelf. He made it to the changing rooms, darted into a cubicle, pulling closed the curtain and yanked off his clothes. His T-shirt and shorts arced over the wall into a neighbouring cubicle.

He pulled on the jeans and white shirt, then, looking in the mirror, pulled the baseball cap tight and low. When he slipped on the reading glasses everything went blurry. Taking a deep breath, he opened the curtain and his vision swam with a twisted grey shape. The top of the monster's head had been sheared off, just like a boiled egg, to reveal glistening brains. It was tall, and hunched over, wearing overalls with a patch reading *Mid West Oil* over his heart.

A lifetime's practice kicked in. Even though his heart felt like it might leap from his mouth, he feigned a nonchalant expression, staring through the monster, as if he was admiring his new clothes in the mirror behind. The monster unrolled a wanted poster and held it up. Stan turned around, checking the cut of his jeans and shirt.

The monster licked its lips and moved from foot to foot. Its exposed brains shone grey and purple under the lights. Maybe it was the change of clothes, the cap shadowing Stan's face or the reading glasses magnifying his eyes - whatever it was, the monster shook his head, satisfied this wasn't his quarry, and moved on. Stan staggered backwards, releasing his breath and thumped down onto the little stool in the corner.

When he moved out onto the shop floor, the monsters were already leaving, spreading the search into the surrounding streets. Weaving his way through the racks of shirts, trousers, underpants and socks, avoiding the few remaining grey bodies, he headed for the exit.

"Not so quick." A firm grip dug into his shoulder.

Stan spun around, trying to pull free, expecting to see red eyes glaring at him, but instead finding the hand belonged to a portly security guard.

"Hold on Sonny-Jim, I don't think you've paid for any of that gear have you?"

Stan laughed with relief.

"This isn't a joke you know," said the security guard.

Suddenly another pair of arms engulfed Stan.

"Nice one, Terry," said the first security guard looking over Stan's shoulder then. "The manager's office and a little chat with the police for you."

"Whatever," said Stan, watching the last monsters leaving the store.

The store's manager called the police and the police called his mum. There were tears and shouted words. The police tried to persuade the manager to let Stan off with a warning as it was his first offence, but he insisted on Stan being charged.

"It's a slippery slope, son," said an officer with kind eyes, at the police station. "One thing leads to another. Theft to a Young Offender Institution, YOI to drugs, drugs to more theft, theft to prison. Slippery slope, like I say. You don't want to end up like one of them soulless monsters roaming the street do you."

"No, I don't."

"Try to be a good boy then."

His mum took him home. There were more tears and strong words.

"And what the hell have you done to your hair! Please tell me that this isn't something to do with one of Kalina's stupid YouTube films, you promised me."

He shook his head.

"What then?"

"Girls."

"Girls!"

"Yes," he said defensively. "It looks cool."

"Stupid boy. Don't you care about anything?" she said. "You'll have to live with what you did today for the rest of your life."

"I doubt it," said Stan, truthfully, but that was the final straw for his mum.

"Get to your room now!"

At midnight the world reset and the next day was yesterday. His encounter with the police had never happened, he wasn't going to court.

He was no closer to finding Gabby.

# 9

"I could have been a film star, don't you think, Miss Scorsese?" said Enzo, planting his fists on his hips and striking as heroic a pose as a short, balding man of sixty years, with a belly stretching his checked-apron to bursting point, could.

Kalina raised her eyebrows at Stan, then screwed up her face as she slowly appraised Enzo.

"A film star?" said Kalina.

"Yes, me," said Enzo lifting his chin a little higher.

"No."

"No?" Enzo sounded crestfallen.

Now you'll say *why not?* thought Stan, sucking on his milkshake.

"Why not?"

*Because you're too short.*

"Because you're too short," said Kalina.

*Too short?*

"Too short?" Enzo stood on his tiptoes, still not managing to rise much above five feet and a couple of inches.

Stan chewed his milkshake's straw, tasting blood as it dug into his gum. For days he tried the same tactic: change your disguise, move confidently amongst the monsters and don't reveal yourself until you're 100% sure it's Gabby. Still he didn't find her and her parting words were eating him alive.

*'Cause Moses is a liar. You aren't a threat to Death. You're his heir and the only hope we've got of saving him.*

He retreated to Kalina's company and Enzo's cafe. The days ran into one another, looping round and round. However he tried to divert Kalina and Enzo with new topics, the repeated day would eventually pull them back to the script.

*Here comes Mickey Rooney and the iPhone*, thought Stan.

"Mickey Rooney was short," said Enzo.

"Who's Mickey Rooney?" said Kalina.

"He's famous, very famous. Old now but he's been making films for many years. You must have heard of him, even in Poland?"

"Wikipedia," said Kalina getting out her iPhone. "When are you going to get WiFi in here Enzo?"

"WiFi? You know what I call WiFi?"

*Web is for idiots?*

"Web is for idiots, that's what I call it."

"Mickey Rooney, here we go," said Kalina tapping and stroking the iPhone screen. "Wow, he did make a lot of films. I couldn't name one. What about you Spielberg?"

"His first film was Orchids and Ermine in 1927. Other notable films include National Velvet 1944, Baby Face Nelson 1957, It's a Mad, Mad, Mad, Mad World 1963, The Black Stallion 1978 and my personal favourite The Care Bears Movie 1985. Of course, that was voice only," said Stan.

Open mouthed, Kalina and Enzo looked at each other. Kalina checked her screen.

"How do you know that?" she said, shaking her head, setting her bramble-bush hairstyle wobbling.

Stan sniffed and pointed at the radio. A DJ was rabbiting on about his holidays. "The next song will be *Hey Jude*, by The Beatles."

"Spielberg has become a mystic,' said Enzo.

The DJ stopped talking and *Hey Jude* started to play.

Stan pointed across the cafe to an elderly couple enjoying fat slices of cake. "That man's about to drop his fork. When he picks it up he'll say *there's more hairs on this than my head.*"

On cue, the man's arthritic fingers fumbled his fork and it clattered onto the floor. Slowly, he bent over to retrieve it. He slipped on his glasses and inspected the tines.

"More hairs on this than my head," he said laughing.

"The woman behind me is about to cough," said Stan.

She coughed.

"Stan, you're scaring me," said Kalina.

"You're about to say, *me too*, Enzo."

"Me too," said Enzo.

"Stan, how did you do that?" Kalina was frowning. "Stan? Stan … ?"

Stan wasn't listening. On the pavement, on the opposite side of the road, stood Gabby. She was watching him.

"Stan, what?" said Kalina, as he leapt up from his seat.

He burst onto the pavement and Gabby disappeared down an alleyway between two shops on the other side of the road.

"Wait!" he yelled. He dashed into the road, holding out his hands to slow the traffic. A taxi driver shouted abuse. An old woman, who could barely see above her steering wheel, juddered to a halt and hit her horn.

He bounced off the alleyway's wall as it curved right and ran behind the shops, parallel to the high street. It was strewn with half crushed cardboard boxes, broken pallets and empty food tins. A row of half a dozen, wide-mouthed, six feet high cylindrical dustbins stood guard. They stunk of fish, rotten vegetables, vinegar and cat pee.

Gabby was waiting for him; grey skin, bloodshot eyes, crooked limbs. The hem of her faded smock flapped in the breeze. Her torso leant forward at an unnatural angle, as if she'd been blown forward by a hurricane and never recovered.

"I told you to stay hidden! What're you doing in a cafe in the middle of the bloomin' high street?"

"Looking for you. I need answers."

"You *need* to stay hidden, that's what you need. Unless you fancy being heartseeker kebab."

"Why did you say I'm Death's heir? What's that supposed to mean?"

"I'm not doing this now. Moses is nearby, you need to skidaddle. Go home. Stay hidden."

Stan looked around, grabbed a length of broken pallet and whacked it against one of the big dustbins. A gonging sound filled the alleyway.

"We're over here Sergeant!" he shouted, hitting the dustbin again. "Come and get us."

"He'll hear! Stop it!"

"Well, answer my questions." Stan raised the plank again.

Gritting her teeth, Gabby cocked her head, listening. "I fought you'd be better than this. I heard what happened in town, you know. That big shop. You're lucky you ain't dead already."

Her disappointed tone cut through Stan's red mist. He tossed aside the piece of pallet.

"Look, all I want is to understand what's happening to me. I don't understand any of this. Anyway, I don't think I *can* die. A van came straight at me; that close it was," said Stan holding his palm close to his face. "It couldn't have missed me but look, here I am, nothing happened."

"You can't die a *normal* death. Time's been suspended. Didn't you notice that? A normal death won't get you, but Moses will. Or one of his armbands."

Stan stepped forward, pressing his hands together, pleading. "Why did you say I was Death's heir?"

Gabby sighed. "Because it's the truth."

"There's no such thing as Death. Not like a person anyway."

"Yes, there is."

Stan shook his head again.

"What do you think I am?"

"A monster."

Gabby pressed her lips together. "We're not monsters."

"What are you then?"

"Deathlings."

"*Deathlings?*"

"Death's helpers. We collect souls when people die and make sure they reach Forever."

"Helpers? You're murderers. I saw one of you kill my dad. I've seen you kill other people too."

"They weren't killing nobody. They were saving them."

"Liar."

"It's the troof. The universe decides when it's time for somebody to die, not us. Death tells us when it's going to happen and we make sure we're there to save their soul. Otherwise that precious ball of light would float away and poof!" she said bringing her hands together and then letting them float apart. "The soul would break up and be lost. Forever."

"No, no, no. This is madness. Why's Moses calling me the Seer? Why does he want to hurt me?"

Gabby cocked her head again. There were people, or deathlings, shouting in the street nearby. She stared at Stan and licked her lips, weighing up the pros and cons of some internal debate.

"Okay, if I give you answers, do you promise to do what I say and stay out of sight?"

Stan crossed his heart. "Promise."

Gabby spoke quickly. "We always knew that Death wouldn't be with us always, even he'd have to pass to Forever eventually, and Moses wanted to be his heir. He wanted to be the next *Death*. For years it looked like he would be. He was a loyal aide. They were friends. Then fings went wrong. As far as most deathlings know, thirteen years ago, Death suddenly fell into a mysterious coma. Moses is claiming that the coma was caused by a creature he called the Seer being born. Only by killing the Seer could we bring Death back from the coma.

That ain't the troof. The troof is that thirteen years ago *you* were born. Death's son. His true heir. Moses saw his chance to be the next Death disappearing and he wasn't having that. Not after all that time. Not after dreaming about all that power. So he betrayed his friend. He used magic to put Death into the coma and dreamt up the Seer story so he could hunt for the one person who could stop him taking the throne - you. He tried to kill you and your mum back then, but your mum fled into hiding. He killed babies all across the country trying to get you, but she kept you safe. Kept you hidden and on the move. Even kept you safe from those of us who found out the troof and wanted to help you. Wanted to serve you. We call ourselves The Resistance. For all your life we've been searching for you, but we couldn't find you. Your mum did too good a job. Everything changed when you gave yourself away."

"The monst.. deathling I shouted at in the street?"

Gabby nodded.

"I know who my dad is. Charlie Wisdom." Stan fished his dad's lighter from his pocket. "This was his."

"I don't know nothing about a Charlie Wisdom."

"This isn't real. None of this is real. You're something in my head, just like Jean always said."

"It's real. You know it is. You've always known."

"No."

"Yes."

"Gabby? Girl, where the bloody hell you gotten to?" Sergeant Moses stomped his way down the alley.

"Damn his eyes!" Gabby looked around. The alleyway was a dead end and there were no windows within reach. "In the bin. Don't so much as breathe until I get rid of him and then stay put for half an hour. Let us get good and gone."

When Stan hesitated Gabby flapped her arms, ushering him towards one of the tall cylindrical bins. "Come on, come on!"

Stan had to jump up to grab the lip of one of the bins. His trainers skidded against the slimy surface as he tried to find a toe hold.

"Hurry," hissed Gabby, fishing something from a pocket in her dress and hiding it behind her back.

"What're you doing?"

"Nuffink."

"Is that you, Gabby?" Sergeant Moses' voice boomed out.

Stan hauled himself up, bending his leg at an unnatural angle so he could rest his foot on a handle and boost himself into the bin. He crashed down amongst oily cardboard boxes, empty food tins, fish skins, potato peelings and a couple of inches of black, gloopy mess. He could feel it soaking onto his jeans. The gut-twisting, acrid stench of rot filled his nostrils. He had to swallow rapidly to stop himself gagging or even puking. As Sergeant Moses' boots crunched by, he lay still, careful not to upset the rubbish around him, even though a serrated tin lid was cutting into his thigh.

"Hello Sarge," said Gabby.

"It's *Sergeant Moses*, you grubby little tyke. What you doin' hiding away back here? Any decent fella, with a suspicious mind, might think you was up to mischief."

Half a metre above Stan's head, a finger-thick hole had been punched through the bin allowing a beam of sunlight inside. Carefully, he pushed until his right eye was level with it.

"Well, is you up to mischief?" Sunlight flashed on the dagger hilts.

"No."

"No *Sergeant Moses*."

"No Sergeant Moses."

"Well, what is you doin'?"

Gabby brought out the hand hidden behind her back. She was holding an old-fashioned pipe.

"Smoking?"

Gabby nodded.

Sergeant Moses stared at her, licked his lips and sighed. "I know you's already dead child, but it's a god awful habit. Especially for children."

"I'm a hundred and fourteen."

"Only in years," said Sergeant Moses taking a step back from her. "But I'm glad you ain't up to anything nefarious like. Been whispers, there has, from some of my men. That you's in cahoots with the resistance. Same as your rotten-apple of a brother. If that was true, I'd be sorely troubled. Understand what I'm saying?"

"Black sheep, my brother. I'm right behind you Sergeant."

"Might keep you in front of me for a while. 'Til I'm sure of you again. Get what I'm saying?"

Gabby nodded.

"Good. Let's go and find this damn Seer."

As they turned to leave, Stan inched his leg clear of the lid cutting his leg. That was all it took to upset the precarious balance within the bin. A Coke can rolled down the heap of trash and gonged against the side.

He froze, holding his breath as Sergeant Moses spun on the spot.

"Hello, what have we 'ere?"

"Cats. Come on, let's go," said Gabby, grabbing Sergeant Moses sleeve.

He yanked himself free, showing brown teeth as he snarled. He grabbed the broken pallet plank. "You better not be lying to me."

"I'm not lying."

He moved to the bin next to Stan's. Reaching up and over the bin's rim, he stabbed the plank downwards, grunting as he did so. He waggled it around and set the bin ringing.

"Here kitty, kitty! Come out, come out wherever you are."

"Sergeant. There isn't anything in the bins. We're wasting time."

"Shut it," he's said pointing the plank at Gabby, before moving onto Stan's bin.

The first thrust missed him. The second one caught him a glancing blow on the forehead. He bit his lip to stop himself making a sound and tasted blood. The plank descended again, smacking him on the chin.

"There's something big in 'ere," said Sergeant Moses. "I need a closer looky-see." He grabbed a rusty bucket, set it down alongside the bin and hauled himself up.

Stan was paralysed. It was all over. Nowhere to run to. Nowhere to hide. He prepared himself for the look of joy that would spread across Sergeant Moses face when he saw his prey. Instead, there was a loud crunch as the bucket gave way beneath the deathling. Cursing, Sergeant Moses stumbled backwards clattering into another bin and setting it rolling across the alleyway on squeaky wheels. Hissing, a cat scrabbled free of the bin, sprinted down the alley and hurled itself at a fence, claws scrambling for purchase.

In the blink of an eye, a heartseeker was out of Moses' chest and flying down the alley. It pinned the cat to the fence.

"See? Cats! Told you so," said Gabby.

"I hate moggies," he said pulling the knife free and letting the cat fall to the ground. He turned to Gabby. "Looks like you was telling the truth, unless you were trying to recruit moggies to the resistance. I need you girl, you got more wits than most of my numbskull men added up. Don't let me down, eh?"

"Never Sergeant Moses."

The deathling gave her a long penetrating look then grunted and turned away. "Come on. We've heard rumours the Seer's been seen on the other side of the city. I'm shifting the search there."

Stan listened to the sound of their steps fading into the city's rattle and hum before he dared to breath again. Then, just to be sure, he waited a few more minutes before hauling himself free of the bin and dropping to the floor. Groaning, he sat with his back against a wall and rubbed his forehead. Blood mixed with black bin-gunk. His jeans were stained and a fish skin was stuck to his arm. He climbed unsteadily to his feet, feeling scratches and bruises across his body. He took a few long breaths and straightened up.

*That ain't the troof. The troof is that thirteen years ago you were born. Death's son. His true heir.*

He blocked out her words.

Madness.

Nonsense.

He started to walk down the alleyway. Gabby had told him to wait for half an hour, but Sergeant Moses had said he was moving the search to the other side of the city. It had to be safe now.

Sweat ran into his eyes as he walked out into the High Street. He rubbed his eyes and they stung from the vinegary gunk on his fingers. He winced, vision blurring. He stopped rubbing and slowly his vision swam back into focus.

Somebody was blocking his path. A red jacket. Black boots. Stan blinked, trying to clear his vision and looked up. Blood filled eyes. A bushy moustache and equally bushy sideburns.

Stan looked at Sergeant Moses, and Sergeant Moses looked back at him.

"Hello Seer." said the deathling.

# PART TWO

# DEATHLINGS

# 10

Before he could react, Stan found himself encircled by eight deathlings wearing three-dagger armbands.

"You didn't really think I believed all Gabby's blather did you? I been watching that alley cat for months. I knew she'd be turned by the Resistance, just like her brother."

Beyond the circle of Deathlings, Gabby was held by two further armbands. She kicked and hissed, trying to pull herself free, but the deathlings - one a headless soldier in khakis, the other a chef with a shotgun blast through his chest - were too strong.

"You're good boy, I'll give you that," said Sergeant Moses, holding his gaze. "I must have seen you in the streets half a dozen times or more and I'd swear on the Virgin you couldn't see me."

Stan spun on the spot. They were all around him. Sergeant Moses was right; there was nowhere to run to. If he tried to dart between them they'd touch him and then … he'd seen what happened to people when monsters ... when deathlings ... touched them.

"Charlie raise the alarm. Let the troops know we've got him."

Charlie was a squat deathling wearing a hunting jacket and riding helmet. His face was crushed flat and showing the clear imprint of a metal horseshoe. He lent back and opened his mouth, lips stretching impossibly so it filled his ruined face. He cupped his hands around the hole and bellowed out a single, deep rumbling note.

*Ooohhhooowww*!!!!!

"Leave me alone. I haven't done anything to you," said Stan.

"Not done anything," said Sergeant Moses, leaning forward. "You've sucked the life from our glorious leader."

"That's a lie. You put him in the coma. You're just using me to cover your tracks."

"Been listening to Gabby's nonsense have you? Just shut your filthy hole, Seer. I've had enough of your prattle."

"Stan, please stop, what're you doing?"

It was Kalina, concern on her face, running up to him, oblivious to the circle of invisible deathlings. All she could see was a demented Stan, spinning on the spot, talking to fresh air.

Instinctively, the deathlings parted to let her through. Stan seized the moment, darting through the gap Kalina had created in the ring of deathlings.

"Stan!" Her call followed him down the street and so did the deathlings.

He sprinted hard, not daring to look back, skidded into an alley, bounced off the walls. He leapt over a low garden fence, out into a side road and darted between honking cars.

94

Soon his breath came in gasps and a stitch stabbed his side. He couldn't keep going for much longer. He glanced behind. They were closer.

*Ooohhhooowww*!!!!! Charlie's call sounded across the city, summoning more deathlings to the hunt.

Stan's pace began to slow. His lungs were full of fire. His legs were heavy. He couldn't outrun them. Did deathlings even tire? Maybe they'd just keep on running until they fell apart.

He had to try something else. Turning a corner, he leapt behind a low garden wall, pressing himself as close to the bricks as he could, trying to control his ragged breathing.

The clatter of feet arrived seconds later.

"Which way?" one of them said.

"Dunno."

"No way was he that far ahead of us. No way, Jose."

Feet dancing nervously. "We can't lose him, Moses'll flippin' skin us."

"He's hiding. Bet you he's hiding. Search the gardens."

Footsteps spread out across the street. One set headed towards his hiding place. Stan pressed himself tight to the angle of wall and lawn. They'd see him in seconds. It was all over. He was exhausted and there were just too many of them. His mum; they'd find his mum.

"Yoo-hoo, boys! Over here!"

Stan recognised Gabby's voice.

"It's the traitor! Get her!"

Footsteps raced away from his hiding place. The street fell quiet except for Charlie's droning call and the first distant rumble of thunder. Stan lay still filling his lungs with deep breaths.

The deathling's face appeared over the wall, inches from his; grey skin, bloodshot eyes. Stan yelled out instinctively.

"Idiot," said Gabby. "Shut your mouth unless you want them to find you again.  Come on, quick. Follow me."

Stan climbed to his feet, his heart hammering, still trying to catch his breath. Lightning flashed. Thunder boomed a little closer.

"Where to?"

"To save your skin. Again. It's becoming my full time job."

"I didn't ask you to do it."

"Tough, I'm doing it."

By now the streets were full of deathlings, wild-eyed at the thrill of the chase. They'd been hunting the Seer for days, now he was so close they could smell blood. Stan and Gabby moved carefully, diving behind hedges, walls, cars, anything that offered a hiding place from the marauding gangs.

Gabby peered around a fence. "Damn. They've already blocked this street. Do you know any shortcuts to your flat?"

"We're not going back there," said Stan.

"What?"

"I'm not leading them back to my mum."

"You don't have a choice."

"Yes, I do."

"Stan, there are a quarter of a million deathlings in this city and they are all heading towards us. You hear Charlie's call?

That's drawing them like sharks to blood. We can't stay hidden much longer. If we can get back to your flat we have a chance. I know how Moses finks and I've laid down an escape route. If we stay out here, we're dead meat."

"What about my mum?"

"They ain't interested in her."

Stan rubbed sweat from his eyes. "They won't hurt her? You promise."

"They want you. You're the Seer."

They had been so caught up in their argument they hadn't heard the stealthy footsteps behind them.

"Looky here."

They turned to face Sergeant Moses and ten armbands.

Stan and Gabby backed out into the road, keeping their eyes fixed on the deathlings.

Sergeant Moses spat a bullet of ruby red mucus at Gabby's feet. "Traitor."

"You're the real traitor. We know what you did to Death." Gabby jabbed a finger at him.

"Poor deluded girl." Sergeant Moses turned to the armbands. "That's the problem with deathlings dying in their teenage years. They never leave behind their adolescent hysteria. Always looking for a conspiracy they is."

"You know I'm telling the truth."

"The only truth is that to save Death, the Seer has to die and I aim to see that good work completed today."

As the deathlings argued, Stan was looking for an escape route. There wasn't one. If they turned and ran the deathlings would just follow them and wear them down. Terraced houses hemmed them in. Parked cars lined both sides of the road.

He patted a pocket and felt the lozenge shape of his dad's lighter. He slipped his hand into the other pocket and pulled out a handkerchief.

"You can kill me and Stan, but that don't mean the Resistance'll end. There're loads of us. An army and they won't stop until you're gone."

"Stan? First name terms? Got yourself a new boyfriend. Does he like 'em grey and cold?"

The armbands cackled. Gabby glanced at Stan, eyes narrowed in anger.

"He isn't nuffink to me but a way to bring you lot down."

"Lovers tiff already?" said Sergeant Moses.

The deathlings laughed again.

"Seer, what're you doin'?" said Sergeant Moses.

Stan ignored him. He chose an old car. The small, square metal protective door squealed open on rusty hinges. He twisted the petrol cap; old cars didn't have lockable petrol caps. The screw was gummy and rusty and for a heartbeat he thought it wasn't going to move. He twisted it free and tossed it aside.

"I said: What're you doin'?"

Stan scrunched the handkerchief into a ball, but left one corner dangling free. He flicked the lighter into life.

"You ain't got the bottle," said Sergeant Moses.

"Run!" said Stan.

Gabby sprinted after him. After Stan dropped the flaming handkerchief into the petrol tank, there was a couple of seconds delay and then an intense, orange light and a deafening explosion filled the street sending Stan and Gabby skidding in one direction and Sergeant Moses and his armbands in the other.

"Come on," said Stan, clambering to his feet. He had a scrape down one cheek. Gabby was on her feet, moving alongside him in her broken-clockwork run, in seconds.

When Stan looked back, he could see the armbands beating out flames that had consumed one side of Sergeant Moses tunic, then they turned a corner and the deathlings were lost from view.

Lightning flashed and thunder boomed closer by the second as they sprinted down the last couple of streets separating them from his flat. Deathlings blocked their route again.

"Damn."

"This way," said Stan.

He dashed down the alley at the side of the house. Reaching over a gate, he slid back a bolt and dashed into the back garden.

"Oi! What you doing you cheeky little beggar!" said a woman hurriedly unpegging washing from a line.

Stan ignored her. He slid back a couple of fence panels, that were only secured at the top, and squeezed through into the street beyond. Gabby followed him.

"That's handy," said Gabby.

"Lots of bullies around here," said Stan.

It only took them a minute to reach Stan's flat, but the storm was already lashing down by then. He glanced over his shoulder looking for deathlings, key fumbling in the lock, as he tried to open the door. His hair was plastered to his head and rain dripped from his nose.

"Hurry," said Gabby.

*Ooohhhooowww*!!!!!

They could hear the sound of raised voices; a mob heading towards them. The door opened and Stan slammed it closed. They ran upstairs. A clap of thunder sounded directly above the house rattling windows.

"Stan, what happened to your face! And what's all that stuff on your clothes. You stink." His mum was standing on the landing, towelling dry her hair. She dropped the towel, grabbed him by his shoulders and inspected the graze.

"I tripped over," he said.

She sighed. "Fighting again?"

Gabby moved, unseen, past Lucy.

"I *tripped over*, honest. I was running to beat the storm."

Out of the corner of his eye, Stan could see Gabby peering out the front window. If his mum turned around now she'd see the net curtains moving on their own.

"I was running home to beat the storm," he said, snagging her attention again.

"You have to tell me the truth, Stan."

He needed to see what was happening outside. He expected to hear deathlings thumping against the door at any second.

"That's the truth. Cross my heart, hope to die, stick a pin in my eye, and all that."

She cleaned the scrape and dabbed antiseptic cream on it.

"It isn't too bad," she said, kissing him on the forehead. "Honestly, you're going to be the death of me, Stan Wisdom. Now get those stinking clothes off and have a shower."

"In a second. I just need to do something first."

"What?"

"Something."

Lucy sighed and moved into the kitchen. "Teenagers."

Stan walked as casually as he could into the living and took the curtains from Gabby. Side by side, they peered through the rain streaked window into the street. There were already at least thirty deathlings staring back up at them and more were joining every second.

"Why aren't they trying to get in?"

"What did you say?" called Lucy from the kitchen.

"Nothing, talking to myself," said Stan.

Gabby sighed and smiled.

"What?" This time Stan whispered.

"They fell for it. I know Moses. He's cautious. He thinks it's all over you see. He's got us bottled up in here and all he has to do is wait 'til midnight. Wait for the day to reset. They know you won't be able to stay awake. Soon as your eyes close they'll come for you and there won't be anything you can do."

"So what *are* we going to do?"

There were cheers from below as a new group of deathlings joined the throng. Sergeant Moses was at the head of the group. One side of his tunic was seared black. He looked up at the window and smiled.

Lucy appeared at his other side. "What's so interesting down there?"

"Just watching the storm."

"Feels like its hovering right over the flat doesn't it."

"A storm just for us," said Stan.

All three of them fell silent.

Finally Stan spoke. "What do I do now?"

"You do the impossible. You stay awake past midnight. If you can do that I might be able to get us out," said Gabby.

"Get in the shower, you smell of fish," said Lucy.

# 11

Lucy went to bed early with a headache. "I want you in bed by nine, no later, understood?"

"Okay."

"No internet."

"Okay." Stan hugged her tightly.

"Crikey, you're crushing me. I'll still be here in the morning."

"I know."

Lucy held him at arms length, looked him in the eye. "Everything all right? Anything you want to tell me?"

Stan opened his mouth.

"Don't tell her nuffink," said Gabby. "Tonight's gonna be tough enough."

"I'm fine."

"Good." Lucy kissed his forehead and disappeared into her bedroom.

Stan jabbed a finger at Gabby and whispered: "You don't get to tell me what I can or can't say to my mum."

"Want to stay alive? Do what I say."

"I can do this on..." Stan's sentence was swallowed by a huge yawn.

"On your own? I 'fink not. Coffee, now."

Stan did as she said. As he stirred his coffee, guilt tickled his conscience; Gabby had saved him earlier: "Want one?"

"I'm dead. Don't do drinking, nor eating no more."

"So you were alive once?"

"Of course I was alive. Where do you fink I come from, the moon?"

"I don't know. You've never told me. Never told me anything except that you're a deathling."

There was a roar from outside and Stan rushed back to the window expecting to see deathlings rushing the flat. The crowd had swelled even more, filling the street, but they were still a distance from the building. They were jostling for position, pushing and shoving, laughing as a party atmosphere took hold. The hunt was nearly over.

"Sheep," said Gabby.

"Why do you call them that?"

"Because they follow Moses even though they know it's wrong. They're just like people. Live people. They'll follow a strong leader and do bad things and then make themselves feel better by saying they didn't have a choice. They were just following orders. They didn't really know what was going on. They make me sick."

Gabby drew the curtains back and a great, mocking cheer rose from the crowd.

"They were all alive once, every one of them. Alive as you and your mum. Doing a days work, living and loving and getting on with life as best they could. Some of them are new dead. Others from the last century, or the century before that, like me.

104

All the way back in time and from all over the world. All of them was alive, and then their time was up, like everybody's time is up one day."

"Only difference was when their deathling came to save their soul and send it on to Forever, they was terrified. Mortal afraid of the unknown. See, they just wasn't ready to pass on. So Death made them an offer. Instead of passing on they could stay, half way between life and Forever, and become a deathling."

"That's what happened to you?"

"Yes."

"Did it hurt when you died."

Gabby stared at the reflection of her broken body.

"Gabby?"

"It hurt. A lot. I just wanted that pain to stop ... but the light. I remember this great light and the deathling holding my soul in his hands, ready to let it fly towards the light and ... I was so scared. The light was gonna eat me up. I wouldn't *be* no more. I was a girl. I didn't know much about life let alone death and Forever. I wasn't ready."

A bloody teardrop ran down one cheek. She sniffed and rubbed at the tear, smearing it across her cheek.

"Still hurts now too. Curse of the deathlings. Escape the light, but live with the pain at the point of death every day."

"What do you mean?"

Gabby touched her crushed chest. "Feels like I've just been crushed every day."

"No?"

Gabby nodded.

"Every day?"

"You get used to it, sort of. Otherwise you go mad. Lots do.We have to lock them up before they run around taking souls that aren't ready yet. Anyway, I've toughed up. Same as you have to."

"Your arms they're all ..." Stan bent his arms at as unnatural an angle as he could manage. "They must really hurt."

Gabby looked away from him. "I was pretty once," she said.

Stan knew he'd hurt Gabby's feelings but he didn't know how to apologise. He found himself tongue tied with most normal girls let alone one that was dead, or nearly dead, or whatever she was.

"I'm sorry I ..."

"Don't matter no more. That's just how I died. Crushed. Both my arms were broken. So were most of my ribs and they stabbed into my heart and lungs. You learn a lot about ways to die when you become a deathling. I'm a Crumple: my job is to collect the souls of those who die like me. Car crashes, falling off buildings, industrial accidents, that sort of lovely stuff."

She parted the curtains and pointed down at the mob. They jumped up and down, laughing scornfully and hurling insults. Gabby ignored them.

"See the really thin ones, all withered and wrinkled? We call them Twigs. They collect the old. Smoke coming out the mouth and burnt flesh? They're Candles. Gunshot and knife wounds? Murders. The fat, blue-veined ones that spurt water? Floaters. They collect the drowned. See that one?"

106

Stan looked where she was pointing. A leg-less torso floated in midair.

"That's a Scattering. Explosions. Don't see many of them."

"What are the ones covered in boils?"

"They're the Pox. Disease and plague."

The deathlings fell silent as Sergeant Moses moved to the front of the crowd. "Seer! Show yourself boy."

"Ignore him," said Gabby.

Stan couldn't ignore him. It was his code; he had to stand up to bullies. He stepped close to the window.

Sergeant Moses pointed at Stan. "I see you Seer. We all see you, don't we?"

The crowd jeered.

"You're trapped just like rats should be trapped. No way out. Give yourself up and I'll make your end swift."

Stan shook his head. It felt heavy and awkward. Sergeant Moses' blood filled gaze held him in a firm grip.

"Good," he purred the word. "I was hoping to play this game to its end. That way you get the treatment what you deserve. Are you feeling tired yet? Heavy headed? Eyelids drooping? Yawning every few beats of your cowardly heart?"

Stan turned his head but it didn't move. His vision blurred. All that existed were Sergeant Moses' eyes. His words. A sudden urge to seek the comfort of sleep.

"Sleep's coming. Deep sleep. Can you feel its arms pulling you down? Holding you tight? Give in to it."

Somewhere, far away, Gabby was shouting about hypnotism; shouting at him to open his eyes.

His eyes were open?

Sergeant Moses' voice rumbled on. "While you're in that deep sleep, we'll kill your little helper, and mother. Then, ah, then it's an end for you. A deep, dark, eternity of nothing. Can you imagine that. Nothing for eternity? Try it. See if you can feel the flutter of terror in your heart."

*Stan*! The voice was miles away, shouting through mountains of cotton wool. *Wake up!*

A sudden, cold shock. His eyes opened. His was standing by his bed pulling back the quilt. Water dripped from his face. Gabby was standing in front of him with an empty glass in her hand.

"You've got to fight it. Don't listen to another word from Moses. He's trying to hypnotise you. More coffee."

Stan drank another sludgy cup of coffee and paced the flat. Caffeine raced through his body. His hands started to twitch. His eyes felt gritty. Gabby wouldn't let him sit. *You rest and sleep'll take you.* At ten thirty he woke to find himself climbing into bed as Gabby whacked him across the face with a pillow. The bed and his torso were soaking wet from water she'd thrown over him.

More coffee. More pacing. More siren threats from Sergeant Moses. *Don't listen*, pleaded Gabby. Stan's caffeine-fired nerves were jumping like popcorn in a frying pan, but his eyes refused to stay open.

He woke in his bed. The room was dark. A deep throated laugh. Sergeant Moses slid from the shadows, pulling heartseekers from his chest. Blood oozed down his tunic and dripped from the blades.

"It was always gonna end this way," he said, raising the knives and plunging them into Stan's heart.

Stan woke again. He was in bed, beneath the covers. Gabby was crouched down in front of him, yelling into his face. He crawled from the quilt. Looked at the clock: 23:45.

"Just fifteen minutes," she said. "On your feet. Come on. You can do it."

Stan slapped his face as he staggered around the room. Outside the deathlings were singing a song that sounded like a hymn. Stan couldn't form clear thoughts. The room pitched and rolled like a ship in a storm. Somewhere nearby he heard a thump and then the squeal of tinny metal grating against itself. What was it? A sound he knew?

He slipped to his knees, eyes closing and energy draining from his body. "I can't do it."

Gabby was in front of him again. Holding something at his eye level. "You can. If you don't you've kissed your mum for the last time. Look."

Stan's eyes were closing again. His vision cloudy. Raising an eyelid was the hardest thing he had ever had to do.

"Look!" snapped Gabby. Light hit his iris. Wobbly green light. His bedside clock: 23:59.

"One minute."

It was too late; a monumental wave of fatigue crashed down over him, obliterating his resolve. He closed his eyes.

Sleep took him.

# 12

Down he fell. Down into the iron grip of deep sleep. It pulled him close. But not even the tightest of vices can hold smoke and so it was with Gabby's last words. They curled through Stan's mind, evading sleep's clutches.

*You can do it. If you don't you've kissed your mum for the last time.*

*His mum ...*

He wouldn't abandon his mum. He was Stan Wisdom, he didn't give in to bullies. He clung to this thought like a rope dangling down into a dark well and started to haul himself up towards a pinprick of light.

A distant voice was calling his name. Somebody sobbing. He pulled harder. The pinprick of light became a coin, a football, a manhole and he opened his eyes. He sat up, gulping deep breaths as if he had been holding his breath under water.

Gabby was slumped against the wall, bloody tears streaking a face that was suddenly brightened by a smile so beautiful as to be totally at odds with her deathling form.

"You did it," she said wiping away tears.

"Time?" said Stan, struggling against a new wave of tiredness.

Gabby held up the clock and 00:00 changed to 00:01. In an instant the fatigue vanished. Any elation Stan might have felt was snuffed out by the cheer that rose outside.

"They're coming. Quick." She waved a hand, beckoning him out onto the landing. The loft door had been opened and its ladder unfolded. That had been the screeching he heard amidst his delirium.

"Up," said Gabby.

Stan ignored her. He dashed into his mum's room and shook her. "Wake up!"

"Nobody wakes until morning. We have to go now."

Heavy thuds sounded from downstairs as the deathlings attacked the front door.

"I'm not leaving her for them," said Stan shaking her again. There was no response. Her body flopped around like a doll.

"They're not interested in her. It's you they want."

"I heard him just now in the street," said Stan. "He said he'd kill her."

"They're not gonna hurt her while you're free. They'll want to use her to get to you. If they take both of you, you can't help her at all. Can you? Think!"

The front door crashed open and the mob of deathlings surged inside and set about the door to Stan's flat.

"Come on!" Gabby was clambering up the ladder.

"If we leave her will they take her?"

Gabby nodded.

Stan ground his teeth and kissed his mum on the forehead. "I'll rescue you. I promise. I won't let them win."

The door started to break apart. The deathlings' excited cries sounded like they were already in the flat. Stan followed Gabby into the loft, smacking his knee against a rung, then hurriedly hauled up the ladder. It snagged on its rusty rollers.

"Quick," said Gabby.

"It's stuck."

Downstairs, wood splintered and cracked as the deathlings burst into the flat.

"Come on!" Stan leant back, pulling with all his strength. Squealing and grating on its runners, the ladder lurched up into the loft.

"The cover," said Gabby.

Stan lowered it into place as deathlings surged down the corridor in a wave of grey skin. The loft was dark except for a slim square of light around the edge of the cover.

"Bring 'im to me fellas," said Sergeant Moses.

The deathlings spreading out through the little flat.

"It's here! The mother!" screeched a high pitched voice.

Deathlings crowded into his mum's room, directly below them. Stan could hear them cackling and hurling insults at her. Somebody hawked and spat.

"Kill it now!" a female voice.

It was too much for him. He reached for the cover, hooking his fingers under the lip.

"Open that and she's dead. So are we." Gabby leant forward, holding down the other side of the cover.

They stared at each other in the dim light.

"Do you promise me they won't hurt her if I escape?"

Gabby didn't hesitate. "Yes."

"If you're lying to me...."

"I'm not."

"Wrap her up and bring her downstairs," said Sergeant Moses, growling. His heavy steps thumped around below. "Now find me the Seer. I want him, and that traitor. Rip the place to pieces. They're hiding somewhere. Under the beds, wardrobes, behind curtains, in cupboards. I want them!"

"Follow me," whispered Gabby.

She pulled a torch from a box and flicked its beam across the loft. About twenty bricks had been removed from the wall to open up a hole into the neighbour's loft. Stan peered through the hole into a space cluttered with cardboard boxes, cobwebs, an old lawnmower, half a bike, rusting radiators and a thousand other forgotten things.

"I heard you doing this, but I thought I was dreaming," he said.

"Forward planning." Gabby raised the torch to illuminate a similar hole in the next wall along, and then another and another; a route that meant they could pass four houses down the road.

"Where are they?" shouted Sergeant Moses, smashing crockery. A deathling yelped. He was hurling plates at them. Footsteps thumped down the corridor. "There's a loft here you idiots. Anybody checked that? Well? Do I have to think of everything myself? Get up there now."

"Come on," said Gabby, gritting her teeth as she bent her twisted limbs to new extremes climbing into the next loft.

Stan followed her. Behind him the loft cover lurched up, throwing shafts of light into the darkness, then clattered back down.

"On his shoulders," shouted Sergeant Moses.

They made it to the fourth loft before the deathlings made it into the first. "Ah! There's a hole in the wall!" shouted a deathling and Sergeant Moses bellowed something they couldn't hear clearly.

Gabby pulled up a loft cover and manoeuvred herself into the hole. She dangled by her finger tips and then crashed down onto the dark landing below.

"You okay?" said Stan.

"Yes, hurry."

"Just asking."

"Try just hurrying."

Stan dropped down alongside her. Gabby led the way downstairs and into the kitchen. The sound of pursuit echoed from above. Gabby flicked on the kitchen light and looked at a key rack. "Blue tab, blue tab, blue tab," she said scanning the keys. "There!"

She grabbed a key and opened the back door. The night air was cool after the long night in the flat, but any comfort was offset by the sound of pursuit. Orders were being passed down the line. The deathlings knew Stan and Gabby were no longer in the house and were moving towards them, garden by garden, some struggling, others slipping over fences as sinuously as cats.

"Come on!" said Gabby, scrabbling over a fence and dropping down into the facing garden. Stan hauled himself up and over after her. A yell went up from the pursing deathlings as he was backlit by moonlight.

They sprinted down the garden, alongside the house, burst through its side gate and out into the road.

"Where are you?" Gabby was looking left and right. "Where the hell are you?"

"Who?"

Gabby ignored him.

Masses of deathlings rushed into the street from both ends, pushing and jostling, desperate to be the first to reach Stan and Gabby.

"They were meant to be here."

The deathlings were closing in, the least damaged ones leading the charge. The rest, rocking and jerking, hurried behind.

Stan balled up his fists. He knew there was no point in running. There were just too many of them. It was time to make a stand.

"I'm sorry," said Gabby. "I had a *plan*."

"You tried."

"Trying isn't good enough."

"You any good at fighting?"

Gabby looked at Stan as if he'd mortally offended her. "I'm a girl. I don't fight. Well, not unless I'm in a pickle."

"We're in a pickle."

"Maybe not!" said Gabby, her voice brightening at the sound of screeching tyres.

At the far end of the street, a battered car with mirrored windows swung into view. It roared towards them scattering deathlings. Acrid smoke rose from its back tyres as it skidded to a halt alongside Stan and the back door opened on squealing hinges.

"In now!" said a deep voice.

Gabby leapt inside and Stan followed her, slamming the door behind him.

Stan found himself staring at a scattering; nothing more than a pair of eyeballs floating above the passenger seat. Next to them, a heavily veined, blue-skinned floater sat behind the steering-wheel.

"Stan, say hello to Blink and Clifford," said Gabby.

"Hold on tight," said a deep voice that came from where a mouth should have been beneath the floating eyeballs.

"Aaaagh!" yelled the floater, water spewing from his mouth, as he slammed his foot onto the accelerator and the car shot forwards.

Deathlings thudded against the bonnet and spun up and over the speeding car. A skull smacked the windscreen and cracks webbed the glass. The floater swerved back and forth trying to dislodge a twig clinging to a wing mirror. It looked ancient, with wrinkles upon wrinkles, its gummy mouth worked soundlessly. The car lurched to the left, scraping against a garden wall. When it jerked back into the road the twig was gone but its severed hand still clung to the wing mirror.

"That'll come in handy," said the eyeballs, laughing and glancing back past Stan. "We're clear, slow down, Cliffy."

Stan looked out the back window. Deathlings were still chasing them, but quickly receding into the distance. When the car screeched onto the main road, back wheels sliding around behind them in a rubber-burning arc, they were lost from sight.

"I said slow down!" shouted the eyeballs.

"I heard what you said, Blink. Heard you the first time. Loud and clear I did. *Slow down* you said, *we're clear*," said the Floater, gripping the wheel so tightly his already prominent veins looked like they had been plumbed into the outside of his skin.

"Well? Slow down then!" yelled Blink.

"Clifford, please," said Gabby leaning forward, putting a reassuring hand on the floater's shoulder.

He released a long, slow, watery breath and decelerated.

"Hallelujah," said the eyeballs.

In the instant they swept past his street, Stan pressed his face to the glass. The deathlings were carrying a body shaped bundle, swaddled in blankets, from his flat.

"No," he growled, pulling on the door handle. Nothing happened. He yanked it up and down.

"Child locks," said Blink. "They're handy as well."

"Let me out," he shouted.

The eyeballs swivelled to face him. For the first time, Stan saw long veins dangling from the back of the eyes. "No."

Stan was eyeball to eyeball with Blink.

"Stan," said Gabby.

Stan turned to face her.

"We'll get her back. I promise."

Street lights illuminated the car with momentary splashes of orange. Stan growled as he yanked at the door handle again.

"What's he doing?" said Clifford, twisting his head.

"Eyes on the road," said Blink, then turned his attention back to Stan. "Calm down kid, you're scaring aqua boy."

"No, you calm down." Stan spun to face the three deathlings and thrust an arm between the front seats reaching for the steering wheel.

Gabby screamed at him to stop. Blink swore. Clifford wrenched the steering wheel to the side. The car jolted violently as it hit a high kerb and they were flying. Stan saw pavement as sky and a starry sky as pavement. A shop front twisted by in a neon blur. Stan's jaw whacked into the back of Clifford's headrest and his vision darkened. Somewhere Gabby and Blink were shouting. Metal crunched and shrieked. Glass shattered. Stan felt pressure on his neck. His body weight pressing down on his neck. How could that be? A wheel spinning, slowing, ticking to a stop.

Darkness.

Silence.

# 13

The room was dark. Why was he in a room? He should be in a car. His mum? They had his mum. He had to rescue her. He tried to get up. He didn't. He tried to move. He couldn't.

The darkness returned.

*

He woke again. The room was lighter, but still in shadow. Heavy curtains covered a high window allowing only a slim, rectangular band of light access at its perimeter. He was lying in bed beneath a quilt. Next to him was a bedside table. A glass of water. No clock. Opposite, an old-fashioned wardrobe, doors ajar revealing an empty belly. The room smelt unused, musty. There was a bandage wrapped around his forehead and it was crusted with blood. Sharp pain zigzagged temple to temple as he probed it for wounds. A shadow at the foot of the bed. Moving towards him. He had to move. Now. He closed his eyes. He'd only rest for a second. He slept for hours.

\*

"Wake up."

The voice was somewhere high, overhead.

"Stan? Are you awake?"

He struggled upwards against the dead weight of fatigue.

"Stan."

He opened his eyes. The lashes were gummed together. His vision cloudy. He rubbed them clean and blinked. He was still lying in the bed. Gabby was sitting on a chair alongside him.

"What happened?" he said. His voice was dry, croaky.

"Drink," said Gabby.

Wincing, Stan propped himself upright with a pillow. Every inch of his body was aching. He felt like the Collins brothers had beaten up on him for an afternoon. He touched his forehead. A bandage had been wound around his brow. He thought he'd dreamed it.

"You wouldn't believe how hard it is to put on a bandage when you can't bloomin' well touch somebody," said Gabby.

"You did this?"

"She hasn't left your side for forty-eight hours," said a deep voice from the other side of the bed. Stan turned and winced. Blink's eyeballs were just visible in the shadows. "I think she's sweet on you."

"Shut up, you idiot," said Gabby.

"I thought he already had a girlfriend. You know, the one with weird hair."

"Kalina's not my girlfriend," said Stan.

"See, you're in with a chance," said Blink.

"Blink, shut up or get out."

"What happened," said Stan.

"What happened? You made us crash, that's what happened. It was lucky we were so far away from Moses' mob otherwise they would have had the lot of us." The eyeballs floated closer, veins dangling. "That was a stupid ..."

"Enough," snapped Gabby. "He was just trying to save his mum. We all do crazy things for the people we love."

"He's got more to worry about than her."

"He will do."

"When? He's got responsibilities."

Gabby jumped to her feet and pointed at the bedroom door with a crooked arm. "When I decide. Now leave me with him. Check on Clifford."

"We have to do something soon. There aren't many of us left." Blink floated towards the door.

"Out!"

"He's supposed to be Death's son. I was expecting some of his father's fire. A leader. Somebody I could follow. Somebody to get us out of this mess."

"Out!"

He slipped out the room and disappeared into the gloom of the landing.

"Why do you all keep saying I'm Death's son? It's nonsense. I'm just Stan Wisdom. I'm just a boy."

Gabby sighed. "If you're just a boy, how come you can see deathlings?"

"Maybe you aren't real. Maybe all the kids are right and I'm mad. I don't know. Just because I see you doesn't mean that I'm Death's son. What proof do you have?"

"Herne told us."

"Who's Herne?"

"He's one of the oldest Deathlings. A Druid. An ancient tree magician, from back when the Romans were in Britain hunting them on account of them not worshipping the proper gods."

Stan remembered the deathling at Sergeant Moses' rally: Long white hair, green robes, swirling tattoos across his cheeks.

"I saw him. He was *supporting* Moses."

Gabby shook her head. "He's playing at supporting him. Risking his soul for the Resistance."

"Who is he? Why does he think he knows so much about me?"

"Before Moses came along, he was Death's closest advisor. He knows the truth of what happened back then."

"What truth?"

"I don't know if you're strong enough for this yet," said Gabby.

"Just tell me whatever it is you think you know about me."

"Suppose you have to hear this eventually." Gabby stared at him. "Death isn't like the rest of us. He isn't all broken and grey. He can make himself visible to humans and even touch them without taking their soul. He could almost be a man again. One day, he told Herne he had done what all men do. He'd met a beautiful woman, fallen in love and made a baby."

"I know who my dad was," said Stan, pushing himself up straight in bed. "He died when I was three. In a supermarket. I saw it happen. A deathling killed him."

Gabby ignored him. "The only problem was that Death told Moses too. Herne was happy for Death, but Moses wasn't. He just saw his plan to take the throne under threat. For years Death had spoken of how tired he was and how he longed to pass on to Forever. Moses had manoeuvred himself into a position of influence, he was sure Death would name him successor. But now there was a child. An heir. Suddenly, his plans were in ruins and he was mad as hell."

"Are you listening to me? My dad was Charlie Wisdom." Stan fumbled his lighter from his pocket. "This was his lighter. He gave it to me. I remember him. We went on holidays. He taught me magic tricks."

"I don't know who Charlie Wisdom was, but he wasn't your real father."

"You know nothing about me."

"Death knew that any child of his would be different, powerful. A halfway being, able to live in the human world but to see the kingdom of the deathlings too."

Stan tried to wrestle free of the sheets but his vision swam and pain hammered his temple. "My dad was Charlie Wisdom."

"Moses made his move. No way was he going to be overlooked. For years he'd been learning magic from Death and in secret studying its darkest secrets. Messing around with stuff that should be left in the shadows. Now he had a use for it. He betrayed Death, his friend, who had raised him up to a position of power. He poisoned him and while he lay writhing in agony, unleashed a conjuration that trapped him in the deepest of comas. Moses followers murdered all Death's closest supporters. Herne only survived the purge by pretending to support Moses. He knew he had to buy time to save you."

"I'm not listening anymore."

"Then Moses told the rest of the Deathlings the great lie. Weeping blood he spoke to us. He told us that Death had fallen into a coma and named him his heir. Playing humble, he told us he would only take on Death's powers temporarily, as he fought to rescue his friend from the malady afflicting him."

"It didn't take us long to see just how different things would be now. Moses didn't wait for the universe to tell him who was to die. He ordered new born babies to be killed across the city. Across the country. Most deathlings didn't know what was happening. They just followed orders."

"Doctors didn't know what was happening. They thought it was a new disease. It was Moses. Trying to snuff you out before you had a chance to learn who you really were. You look at the newspapers from back then. You'll see it's true."

"Just because *that* happened, it doesn't mean it had anything to do with me. There has to be another reason I am like I am. Another reason I can see you."

"Like what?"

"Maybe I was bitten by a radioactive spider."

Gabby laughed.

"This isn't funny," said Stan. "You're standing my life on its head and shaking it until everything falls out."

"I'm sorry, Stan. Maybe you're right. Maybe we're wrong. But I don't think so and while there's a chance that you're who we think you are, that you can wake Death and destroy Moses, I'm going to keep believing in you. Do you know why?"

"No."

"'Cause I was one of those that believed Moses in the beginning. I didn't know better. I sneaked into hospitals looking for new born babies. I did bad things."

Lips pressed together, Gabby stood and walked a jerky circuit of the room. She took a shaky breath and sat down again.

"When I learnt the truth of what was happening, I knew I'd never forgive myself. All I could do to ease my guilt was to make sure I brought him down. Even if I had to die doing it. So you may not believe me, or believe in yourself, but I'm going to keep believing 'cause I ain't got anything else to believe in. All I can ask you to do is trust that whatever I'm doing, it's for the best. Can you do that? Please."

Stan stared at Gabby; at her grey skin, pitted and rough like leather, her bloodshot eyes, her twisted limbs and crushed chest that made her move like an alien. He forced himself to see beyond them to the girl that she once was. He painted her skin a rich flesh tone, the colour of somebody who spends many hours outdoors, with a blush of red on her cheeks. He straightened her limbs and reformed her chest. He cleared her eyes so that inquisitive bright blue irises stared back at him.

"Okay."

"Thank you," she said. "Now, I have to leave for a while. I need to get my orders from Herne."

"What do I do?"

"Recover. Get stronger. Blink and Clifford'll be on guard."

Stan screwed his face up.

"Blink can be an arse, but I'd trust him with me life."

"What's that?" said Stan pointing.

As Gabby stood, bones grating and crunching, a half-coin pendant slipped free from the top of her dress. She held the pendant and smiled sadly.

"Me and my brother, Joseph, have half-'an-half. We sent him to find you days ago, but we haven't heard from him. He's either hiding or Moses' men have got him. If they've got him, they'll be torturing him," Gabby swallowed. Bloody tears glistened in her eyes. "He won't give us up. Not my Joe."

Gabby's words were fading as Stan remembered the deathling in the woods. The memories that had flooded his mind: *a busy street with tall, grand buildings. Men wearing long, black coats and top hats. Walking sticks clicking against the pavements. Women with bonnets and wide skirts. A dark street. Gas lamps. Puddles of light. Horse drawn carriages clattering over wet cobblestones splashing him. A man slashing at him with a walking stick. The sting of polished wood on his skin. Losing his footing and falling backwards, stumbling into the road. A girl's voice. Screaming. Fingers grasping his sleeve. His momentum carrying both of them into the road. Into the path of a carriage and it's iron-shod wheels. Onto his back, the wheels crunching over cobblestones and ...*

"I love him more than anybody."

"You died together?"

Gabby nodded. "Some toff cuffed him with a cane and we both fell under a Hansom cab."

Stan opened his mouth, but didn't speak. He felt the weight of the matching pendant in his jeans pocket.

"Horrible way to die, eh?"

Stan nodded. *How could I have seen that?*

"I'll find him and you'll find your mum. I promise."

He nodded again.

"Try not to cause the boys any bother while I'm gone. I won't be longer than a day. Okay? Get some more sleep. You're going to need it."

"Okay," he said as Gabby rocked from the room.

He opened his mouth to call after her, but closed it again. Guilt burned in his chest. He felt sick and scared.

*How could I have seen that?*

# 14

"Bacon sandwich?" said Clifford as Stan entered the kitchen. The blinds were closed and dust-filled bands of light lit his heavily veined face. The house was hot and stuffy. Stan yawned. He'd slept through the night until ten in the morning.

"Bacon?" repeated Clifford raising the frying pan towards Stan's nose. Water spewed from his mouth as he spoke, vanishing in midair above the hob.

"Please," said Stan, stomach rumbling as he looked around. "Why are all the blinds and curtains closed?"

"Why do you think, Einstein?" A deep voice. Blink floated into view.

Stan ignored him and spoke to Clifford. "I'm going out into the garden."

Clifford glanced at Blink.

"No, you're not," said the eyeballs.

Stan tried the back door but it was locked. "It's boiling in here."

"Sorry. Gabby's orders," said Clifford.

"Gabby, shmabby," growled Blink. "Don't apologise to him. We're saving his skin. They're hunting for him, for all of us, and if they find us, it's over. No mercy. We stay on lock down."

"I need some air," said Stan, rattling the handle.

"No," said Blink.

"Have a bacon sandwich," said Clifford. "I used to love bacon sandwiches."

"Oh don't go all former-life-sentimental again, I can't bear it. It's enough I have to listen to hero-boy's whining."

Stan turned to face Blink. Turned to face those bullying tones. "Don't you miss having the rest of your body. I'm sure it'd come in *handy*."

The frying pat clattered onto the hob and a slice of bacon slithered over the edge landing on the floor with a splat. Clifford's mouth fell open and water dribbled from his lips. "Blink, no."

Blink shot across the kitchen. He stopped inches from Stan. Stan didn't flinch, even though his heart was hammering. He knew how to handle bullies. Show no fear. Face up to them.

"You ever seen an improvised explosive device go off? ... No? ... A bang that'll split your ear drums. Dirt and nails and rocks ripping everything to pieces. The smell of the air burning. Silence ... then screaming. Blood everywhere. Body parts? ... No? ... Ever seen that happen to your friends. Lads only a few years older than you, days into a tour. I died saving idiots like you from an enemy that'd like to do that to all of us. Now I'm having to save you again. Do me a favour, do what I say, when I say it, and don't give me any lip or I might just forget my orders."

Stan swallowed and breathed out as Blink floated from the room. An image of news footage flashed into his mind: a dusty town full of low buildings; men in robes and headdresses; soldiers in uniforms and body armour cradling machine guns; raised voices, a bang then a cloud of dust rising a couple of streets away.

"He was blown up by a bomb. He was only twenty," said Clifford. "He's new to all this. He's worried about Joseph. Gabby's brother. They're good friends and we haven't seen him for days"

Stan swallowed. The pendant felt heavy as a brick in his pocket.

"I'll put on some more bacon," said Clifford.

"Don't bother. Lost my appetite."

*

The day became hotter and stuffier, but still Blink wouldn't even allow them to open a window. Stan tried the windows in the bedroom, but they'd been nailed shut.

He sat on the bed thinking about Joseph. What had happened in that moment he jumped out from the trees? He remembered the feel of the heavy stick in his grip; how he'd lashed out instinctively. The bright light and the vivid images of the old street around him. It had been as if he was there. Then it was over and Joseph was gone. The stick was on the floor and the pendant was tangled around his fingers. There was no other answer. He'd killed Joe.

He pulled the pendant from his pocket. He could just make out the outline of half of a figure, rubbed almost smooth by time. He held it close to his eye. Maybe it had been a Saint Christopher.

"What's that?" It was Clifford in the doorway.

"Nothing," said Stan, quickly stuffing the pendant back into his pocket.

"It was something."

Stan could feel his cheeks colouring under Clifford's scrutiny.

"It was my mum's. Just thinking about her."

"Oh. I bet you miss her."

Stan nodded. He could still feel the weight of Clifford's gaze. He pointed at the thick book of Sudoku puzzles in Clifford's hand, trying to distract him. "I can never do those."

"Well, I have a dark secret. In life I was an accountant. Boring, eh?"

Stan shrugged. "I'm sure it had its moments."

"I'm not."

"Where's Gabby?" he said.

"She'll be back soon."

"Yes, but *where* is she?"

"I can't tell you."

"Please."

"She's meeting Herne."

"I know that. Where?"

"That I definitely can't tell you."

"Worried that I'll go running after her?"

"I'm just following orders."

"Clifford, I can't just stay here, doing nothing, while they've got my mum. I have to try to help her."

Water bubbled from Clifford's lips. "Patience."

"How can I be patient when all this madness is going on around me? I'm not Death's son. You do know that don't you? This is all some crazy mistake?"

"I can't talk to you about that," said Clifford, digging a finger beneath his collar and sliding it around to release the pressure against his swollen neck. He stood up as if to leave the room but Stan blocked the way.

"Says who?"

"Nobody."

"Blink? Do you do everything he tells you?"

"It's for your own good."

"If I'm supposed to be helping you. If I'm supposed to be defeating Sergeant Moses, a little information might help. Come on, Clifford."

Clifford toyed with his tie again, muttering to himself. Water tumbled from his lips. Awkward silence fell on the kitchen.

"How did you die?" said Stan.

Clifford's laugh sounded like water draining out of a bath. "How do you think?"

"I know you drowned, but how? Why?"

"You'll laugh."

"I'm not going to laugh about your death."

Lightning flashed. Thunder rolled through the sky.

"My dog."

"Your dog?"

Clifford sighed, letting out a fine spray of water that lit up like a rainbow as it passed through a beam of light. His gaze had suddenly gone distant. He swallowed water.

"I was walking my dog. She was an English Sheep dog, called Molly. Beautiful dog. Full of life she was. We were in the park and she was chasing her ball. I had one of those plastic ball launchers and I threw it too hard. It went out of the park and skidded onto a frozen canal. It was the middle of winter."

A ruby red tear swelled in the corner of one eye.

"She went onto the ice, fell through and you tried to save her?" said Stan.

Clifford nodded, snuffling up pendulums of bloody snot and wiping away the tears.

"That's terrible. I'm sorry."

The floater fished a handkerchief from his pocket and blew his nose.

Stan wasn't sure what triggered the confession. Maybe it was Clifford's story, maybe it was just the guilt gnawing away at him, but the words came out in a rush.

"I think I killed Joe."

"What?" Clifford glanced at the doorway.

"Gabby's brother, Joe. I think I killed him. Accidentally."

"How?"

"I don't know. Look … I … he surprised me. I had this big stick."

"A stick? You can't kill a deathling with a stick."

"He jumped out in front of me and I lashed out. He was there and then he wasn't. What else can have happened?"

A waterfall was tumbling from Clifford's lips. He rubbed his brow. "Blink can't find out about this. Not until Gabby's back. Are you sure about this?"

"I'm not sure of anything anymore."

The scream came from downstairs, tearing through the threads of their conversation.

"Blink," said Clifford, turning his swollen body and waddling back down stairs and into the living room. Stan followed him. Blink's unfocused eyeballs were floating above the sofa. Another terrified scream ripped through the room. Blink's pupils fluttered, unfocused.

"Blink! Wake up!" said Clifford, halfway between a whisper and shout. "Moses' men might hear."

Blink screamed again.

Clifford was sweating. Water running over his face like a mask. "Blink! BLINK!"

Blink's pupils fluttered again then focused on Clifford. They darted over to Stan then back to Clifford.

"What you looking at?"

"You were having a nightmare," said Clifford.

"So?"

"You were screaming," said Stan.

"So ... I ..." Blink looked back and forth between them then floated out of the room. "You don't know anything."

Clifford tried to form words, but they were lost amidst a watery gurgle. Finally he forced them out. "Poor kid. Not much of an existence being a deathling. Who'd want to live with the pain and memory of their death."

134

"Then why don't you … you know … just die, properly. Pass on to Forever like all the souls you save?"

"It's too late."

"What do you mean?"

"We missed our chance. We chose to become deathlings and now we can never pass to Forever. If we die … *properly* … then its over for us. We just stop being."

"So Joe …"

"I don't think you killed Joe," said Clifford. "I don't know what happened but there has to be another explanation. All I …"

Clifford broke off when the phone rang. He snatched it from its cradle.

"Gabby. Thank god," he said.

"Where is she?" Blink had slid back into the room. "What's going on?"

"Shush," Clifford screwed up his face and waved a hand at the scattering. "Gabby, speak up." He stuffed a fat finger into his ear.

Blink moved alongside Stan as Clifford's eyes went wide.

"Uh huh … Okay … Are you sure … Yes, he's fine … okay … be careful."

Clifford put the phone back in its cradle and turned to them rubbing his lips.

"What's happened?" said Blink.

"Moses' men are tracking her. She can't lose them."

"Damn," said Blink.

"There's something else."

"What?"

"Herne said there's a traitor in the resistance."

# 15

"Where do you think you're going?" said Blink.

Stan ignored him. He left the living room and headed for the front door.

"I'm talking to you!"

"Stan?" said Clifford.

Stan spun to face them. "Gabby's the only one of you I trust. If she isn't coming back, I'm out of here. I'm going get my mum."

"How you going to do that hero?" said Blink.

Stan ignored him and yanked the door. It didn't move. Halfway down were mortice and Yale locks. The top and bottom bolts had been secured with padlocks.

He took a step back and landed a solid kick alongside the locks. The door remained implacable, barely rattling under the impact. He slammed the sole of his foot into it again, channelling his energy down his leg. Again nothing. Gritting his teeth, he attacked it ferociously.

Blink was shouting at Clifford. "Use it. Go on use it now."

"He's a boy."

Stan kicked the door one more time, then panting turned towards the deathlings. "Open it now, or I'm going to start shouting and everybody from here to town will hear."

"Please calm down, Stan," said Clifford.

"Just do it," said Blink.

"Help! Help!"

Clifford pulled a red plastic box from his pocket.

"Use it now!"

Clifford changed his grip on the plastic box and Stan realised what it was. When the floater pulled the trigger, two wires shot out and darts at the tip of each wire embedded themselves in Stan's chest. Suddenly, he was on the floor, body ridged and thrashing, jaw clenched, waves of pain washing through his body.

A Taser, like the police used to subdue violent criminals. They were electrocuting him.

He passed out.

His eyelids flickered open and closed. Clifford had looped a towel under his body and arms and was hauling him upstairs. Stan's head bumped against every step. Clifford cursed. Water tumbled from his mouth. Blink offered advice. The deathlings argued. Clifford stood on the bed, hauling him up with the towel. The door closed. A lock clicked.

His eyes closed.

*

When he came to, it was dark. He had a pounding headache and every muscle in his body ached. He'd bitten his tongue and the lump of healing skin rubbed against his teeth. Dried blood crusted his lips. They'd left him a glass of water and a couple of painkillers on the bedside table. He swallowed them and gulped down the water.

The bedroom door was locked. He rattled the handle, banged on the door and called out to them. Clifford padded upstairs.

"Let me out, now."

"It's for your own good. If you go out there they're going to get you."

Stan thumped he door. "There doesn't seem much difference between you and them to me."

"Sorry." Clifford's footsteps headed back down stairs. "I'll bring up supper later. I'm so sorry."

"Come back!"

Nobody answered Stan's calls after that. He peered through the curtains. Maybe he could call out to a passerby. Claim he'd been kidnapped, get them to call the police; but now his anger had subsided, a nagging fear held him back. Blink was right; what if Sergeant Moses' armbands were in the street? They could be clambering over the rooftops on patrol. They could be anywhere.

He sat on the edge of his bed and thumped the pillow. He could hear Clifford and Blink talking downstairs. He was sick of being lied to. All these years his mum had been protecting him, running from Sergeant Moses, moving from flat to flat; protecting him, but lying to him. Now Gabby was doing the same. She'd said his mum was safe, that she had a plan, but how could any of them be safe when there was a traitor in the resistance.

He realised that the voices weren't downstairs, they were floating up from the front garden. He couldn't hear words, whoever was out there was talking in low tones, but he could sense their urgency. He crept to the window and peeked through the curtains. Heart thumping he jumped back.

"No ... No ... No."

The full moon had offered him a glimpse of the scene below and a glimpse was all he needed. Moonlight lit Blink's eyeballs. Opposite him was a tall, shadowed figure. Stan wouldn't have known who it was except for the glint of moonlight on the knives sticking out of his chest.

He peered out the window again. He was too late. They'd moved to the side of the house. A key rattled in the front door. They were coming in.

Blink was the traitor.

Stan opened the curtains. The big tree moved under a gentle wind. He tugged at the old-fashioned sash window. It wouldn't budge. Six inch nails had been driven through the frames deep into the brickwork.

Voices downstairs. Footsteps climbing towards the bedroom. The stairs creaking. Laughter.

The bedside table wasn't as heavy as Stan expected. He heaved it above his head, staggered on the spot as he fought for balance, then rushed forward and hurled it through the window. Glass shattered, falling in a moonlit shower. The bedside table crunched and burst into pieces.

Feet thundered up the stairs. Voices shouted. Blink's deep tones, Clifford and another.

Stan wrapped a sheet around one hand and punched out the remaining shards of glass.

A key rattled in the lock. *Hurry up you idiot*, said somebody.

Stan backed up to the bed and took a deep breath. The lock clicked. Hinges squeaked. He ran as fast as he could, launching himself head first through the window. For a second, he was in midair, two storeys up, the moonlit garden beneath him. A branch smacked into his stomach, winding him, and he dropped down to a lower branch. Smaller branches and leaves whipped his face. He bounced from branch to branch, unable to grab hold, like a ball in a bagatelle. He scraped his back against bark.

"Stop." Clifford's voice from above.

Stan grabbed a branch and it bent beneath his weight. Twigs and leaves snapped free as he slid down its length. He skinned his palms. The air smelt of sap.

His knees buckled. For a second, he was disoriented, expecting another branch to snap and his fall to continue. He straightened up. He was standing in the garden.

"Get back here you idiot." It was Blink this time.

Stan didn't look back. He didn't see Clifford duck back inside, followed by Blink. He didn't see the third deathling lean out the window; a tall deathling with three cameras strung around his neck. In the moonlight the camera lens flashed almost like metal dagger hilts.

Stan ran into the night and was swallowed by shadow.

# 16

Stan kept running. For a while, he could hear Clifford and Blink calling out to him as they searched the streets, but their voices soon faded. He slowed to a halt and bent over. A stitch gnawed at his side. He winced as he used his teeth to pull a big splinter from his palm.

He looked at his watch. It was 23:45. He didn't feel in the slightest bit tired. He'd broken free of the repeated day. That was one battle he wouldn't have to fight tonight. A few people passed him, walking home, already asleep on their feet. Stan wandered with them, mimicking their zombie shuffle in case a deathling spotted him.

By midnight he was alone in the streets. A shudder ran through the city. It's yesterday for everybody else now, he thought.

He chose a house at random and broke in. Two adults were asleep in one bedroom, a boy about his age in the other. Stan took a hoodie from the boy's drawers. Nobody stirred as it squeaked open and closed. In the bathroom he swallowed two more painkillers and pocketed the rest of the packet. He washed and cleaned his hands, smeared them with antiseptic creams and bandaged them as best as he could.

He made a sandwich and grabbed a bottle of coke then went through to the living room and sat down to eat. There were birthday cards on the windowsill and fireplace: *Happy Birthday Mum; Dear Wife; Happy Birthday Auntie.*

"I'm coming, mum," he said and tears welled up in his eyes. He blinked them away. This was no time for weakness.

He knew he'd have to sit out the night indoors, but tomorrow he'd go back to the safe house. Gabby might not have known that Blink was the traitor and that's where she'd return to if she could lose Moses' men. Stan had to be there to warn her. He knew he needed Gabby if he was to have any chance of rescuing his mum. He set the alarm on his watch for five o'clock, lay down on the sofa and closed his eyes.

\*

"What the hell do you think you're doing! Carol call the police. Hurry. And keep Jimmy up there." The man was shaking him.

As Stan half woke from a disturbed sleep his first thought was that the deathlings had found him. He lashed out and caught the man square on the jaw.

"He hit me! Carol, he hit me!" shouted the man reeling back across the room. Footsteps thumped around upstairs.

A phone keypad beeped as somebody keyed in three numbers. A high-pitched voice shouted. "Police. Yes, police. Hurry, he's murdering my husband!"

"I'm sorry," said Stan waking fully and seeing the reality of the situation. It was the man from the bedroom. Stan had overslept. "Look, I'm going. I didn't steal anything. I just needed somewhere to sleep."

"A police cell will do you nicely," said the man, rubbing his jaw and blocking the exit from the living room. "Looks like you helped yourself to my son's clothes."

"I'm sorry. I had no choice. Just let me go, please."

The man laughed.

"If you don't let me go, you're going to be stuck in this day forever."

"You're going to have to do better than that."

"I'm just telling you what's going to happen if I can't do what I need to do."

The man faced the ceiling and called out. "Are they on the way, love?"

A muted voice said: "Five minutes."

"Please," said Stan.

"You should have thought about the consequences of breaking and entering shouldn't you."

Stan took a step forward and the man raised a fist. "Not so quick."

"Today is the 12th April," said Stan. "I've lived this day twenty times or more and it's never going to change again unless I change it."

The man shook his head and raised his face towards the ceiling. "I think he's on drugs, Carol. You and Jimmy lock yourself in the bathroom."

144

"Today, the Minister for Health is going to resign. There's been a massive mudslide in India that's killed hundreds of people. Barclays are going to make five hundred people redundant. Derby County will knock Manchester United out of the FA Cup in a replay and ..."

There was a clatter as a newspaper was pushed though the letter box. Stan craned his neck to look down the hallway.

"What paper do you read?" said Stan.

"None of your business."

"What paper?"

The intensity of Stan's voice made the man answer. "The Mail."

"Get it," said Stan sitting down on the sofa. "I won't go anywhere. Promise."

"I'm not stupid."

Stan sat on his hands. "Get it. Your family's life depends on what you do before the police arrive."

"Don't know why I'm doing this," said the man shuffling from the room and pointing at Stan. "You so much as twitch and ..."

He dashed out and back in with the paper and stared at the front page: *Indian Mudslide Horror*.

"You could have seen an early edition," said the man.

"Pick a page and ask me what's on it?" said Stan.

"This isn't Mastermind. We're waiting for the police to come and arrest you."

Stan stood up again and the man took a step back. "Ask me."

"Okay, page five."

"There's a story about a British cyclist, Barry Benton, testing positive for drugs and another about how dangerous Britain is compared to twenty years ago."

A siren wailed as a police car raced towards the house.

"Page 8?"

"Archie the Alsatian sitting his A levels and a story about unhelpful doctors' opening hours."

"Twelve?" said the man rustling through the paper.

"*The Hourglass World* is the fastest selling book of all time."

For the first time there was a look of confusion in the man's expression. "Is this some kind of joke? Have the blokes at work put you up to this?"

"No. This is real. You're not in control of your life. Nobody is. You have to let me go. Please."

"You broke into my house," said the man, but he no longer sounded certain of anything. He pointed at Stan's bandaged head. "What happened?"

"Look at the headline on page six," said Stan.

The man found the page and read the headline. "*United Spookdom: Seven out of ten Brits believe in the supernatural.*"

"The seven are right."

The man swallowed. He folded the paper neatly and put it on a coffee table. "I'm going to wake up in a minute, aren't I?"

"Yes," said Stan.

A car screeched to a halt and red and blue lights lit the hallway. Fists hammered on the front door.

"Don't know why I'm doing this," said the man waving a hand towards the back door.

Stan ran. Out the back door, over the back fence and away.

*

It took Stan a while to orient himself. Once he'd found where he was in the city, he headed back towards the safe house. He pulled up his hood and kept his head down. Deathlings were out in force.

He was in a rundown shopping parade, home to hair salons, fast-food stores and charity shops when he saw the girl. She was about his age, with tangled, ash-blonde hair, very pale skin and red-rimmed eyes. Her clothes, a tatty fleece and jeans flapping open at the knee were engrained with dirt. She was sitting on the pavement, her face turned up to passers by, all of whom were passing her without a glance.

"Please help me," she said to a woman in a smart dress and big sunglasses. The woman click-clacked by on high heels.

Next to pass were two youths wearing low-slung jeans and baseball caps. They were too caught up stroking mobile phone screens and giggling at messages to notice her. More people hurrying to work passed without a word and the girl covered her face.

At first, her shouted words were muffled by her hands, but when she moved them away, he heard them loud and clear: "Please ... help me. Monsters ... monsters all around us."

Still none of the passers by stopped to help the girl. If anything, they seemed to speed up as they passed her. She was just another mad, homeless person, probably on drugs; *pass by quickly, don't catch her eye, pretend she's not there.*

"Please," she said imploringly. "They're everywhere, can't you see them?"

Stan couldn't catch his breath. He leant against a wall. *She could see them too?* He took a step towards her then halted, twitching his head from side to side, looking for deathlings.

The girl sobbed into her hands. The sound was like a hook in Stan's heart, pulling him towards her. He knew how it felt to see monsters and for everybody to think you were mad. He'd lived with it most of his life. He could help her and maybe she could help him. Something held him back: his mum, Gabby; he needed to find them. He didn't have time for this.

The girl called out again and still everybody ignored her. Stan couldn't help himself. He crossed the road and crouched down beside her.

"It's okay, I see them too," he said.

She jumped and pulled her hands away from her face, staring at him with terrified eyes. People passed around them but Stan paid them no attention.

The girl sniffed. "Don't mess with me. I'm sick of people laughing at me."

"I'm not laughing at you."

"I don't believe you."

"Cross my heart," he said weaving a finger over his chest.

The girl stared hard at him, as if she was trying to burrow into his brain with her sight. "Honestly?"

"I've seen them all my life. Since I was a little boy. Everybody thought I was mad," said Stan making himself go cross-eyed.

The girl gave a snotty laugh and a brief smile lit her face. "I know how that feels."

"Have you been living rough?"

The girl nodded.

"My name's Stan."

"Louise."

"Are you hungry?"

The girl shrugged.

"You must be. Come on."

He extended a hand to help her up, but she clambered to her feet unaided. She obviously wasn't ready to trust him just yet.

"There's a cafe over the road," he said.

Steam and a wall of greasy heat hit them as they entered the cafe. Bacon sizzled on a griddle. A radio blared out behind the counter. Two pundits discussing last night's football, were abruptly cut off by a jingle.

"Sit on the table by the window,' said Stan. Louise did as she was told.

Stan passed a table where a man was tucking into a pile of eggs and beans. His tattooed arm flipped the paper to the front page: INDIAN MUDSLIDE HORROR.

The big man behind the counter looked suspiciously at Stan from beneath bushy black eyebrows. The name Mohammed was stitched onto his apron. "Ditch the hood, kid."

Stan pulled back his hood and called over his shoulder to Louise. "Cup of tea? Bacon sandwich or full English."

"Sandwich. Please."

"Two bacon sandwiches and two cups of tea please," said Stan.

"Two of each?" said Mohammed, looking at Louise. His eyebrows wriggled like caterpillars.

"I can pay for them?" said Stan showing him a ten pound note.

Mohammed took his money and gave him his change. "Sit down. I'll bring them over."

As Stan returned to their table he heard Mohammed mutter *weirdo*. He ignored him.

"Have you always seen them? Monsters I mean," said Stan, keeping his voice low.

Louise nodded. She opened her mouth, but no words came out. Stan couldn't work out if she was struggling to keep them in or get them out.

"It's okay," he said. "I know, it's hard."

Boiling water hissed from a tap as Mohammed made their tea. Another happy jingle bounced around the steamy room trying to lull people into buying something they didn't need.

"I've been alone for so long. I was adopted. That didn't work out. I had foster parents. More foster parents. They couldn't handle me," she took a deep breath, her mouth wrestling with

150

shapes again. Then she looked Stan in the eyes. "I thought I was mad, did you?"

"A few times," he said nodding. "We're not. I know what the monsters really are."

"What do you mean?"

Stan was about to reply when he sensed Mohammed behind him. He clattered two plates and two cups of tea onto the table in front of Stan. Stan pushed a tea and sandwich across to Louise. "Thanks Mohammed."

"Mohammed?" said the big man.

Stan pointed at the name on the apron.

"That was a bloke that worked here before. Do you really think I look like a Mohammed," said Not-Mohammed shaking his head as he headed back to the counter. "Eat up and go, weirdo."

A couple of the other regulars laughed and muttered to the big man. Stan ignored them and turned his attention back to Louise.

"They're called deathlings."

"Deathlings," she said, leaning forwards, her sore eyes alight with interest.

"Eat," said Stan, as he tore into his bacon sandwich. The cafe might be smelly and greasy, and Not-Mohammed might be a rude idiot, but the bacon sandwiches were great.

Louise shook her head. "I can't eat. My stomach's full of butterflies. This doesn't seem real. I need to know, everything. Please."

Stan swallowed and felt a big ball of bread and bacon scraping its way down his throat. He hadn't realised how hungry he had been. He gulped his tea.

He told her everything: how deathlings collected the souls of the dead; how Sergeant Moses had put Death into a coma and become a dictator; how time has been broken so that the same day repeated itself; how Gabby and Herne were leading a resistance movement to bring down Moses but that there were traitors in the camp.

"Gabby?" said Louise.

"Yes. What?"

"I met her," said Louise, raising her hands, palms open. "Two days ago. I just ignore monsters in the street but she seemed to sense I could see her. I would have run, but I was caught in a dead end street. I thought that was it, I was dead. But she was kind and said she could help me. She said that I should meet her in Brewster Park this afternoon."

Stan started to laugh. Finally his luck was changing. "Today."

"I wasn't going. I thought it was some sort of trick and that there'd be loads of other monsters waiting for me."

"This is brilliant news. Gabby can help us. Where's the park?"

"I dunno. About a twenty minute walk away, I think."

"Hurry up, let's go," said Stan biting off another chunk of sandwich.

"She said she'd be there this *afternoon*."

"So, we'll be early."

As they got up to the leave, Stan pulled up his hood and stuffed Louise's sandwich into his pocket. Not-Mohammed muttered to one of his regulars.

"Want a tip?" shouted Stan.

Not-Mohammed glared at him.

"Lose the caterpillars," said Stan, wriggling his eyebrows.

"Getoutof'ere!" said Not-Mohammed.

# 17

Brewster Park was similar to the park close to Stan's flat only bigger. At its centre was a hillock and Stan and Louise took up a vantage point here, hidden away between two bushes.

On one side of the park was an athletics track fenced in by a graffiti covered fence. On the other, alongside a bridge that ran over a busy train line, a fairground was being set up.

As the morning passed into the afternoon, a Ferris wheel was winched into the sky alongside a helter-skelter. Organ music drifted over the park as waltzers and roundabouts were tested. Carnies yelled out to each other as they effortlessly danced around the whirling machines.

The smell of candy-floss, hotdogs and onions made Stan's stomach rumble, but below these enticing smells was a smokiness he couldn't identify. He offered Louise half the cold bacon sandwich, but again she refused. The longer they stayed on the hill the more nervous she became. She was sitting, hugging her legs to her chest, gently rocking. Her lips constantly moved as she chewed the inside of her mouth.

Distant thunder rumbled; three o'clock, the storm was coming.

"Did Gabby say what time she'd be here?"

Louise shook her head.

"No clue?"

"Just afternoon," said Louise, continuing to rock and chew the inside of her mouth.

"You okay?" said Stan.

She nodded, but there was fear in her eyes. "Don't like to stay in the same place too long."

The fairground opened and kids and families started to stream in. The rides lurched into life and the air rang with music, screams and shouts. Lightning flashed and the thunder stomped across the sky.

Stan stood and stretched, feeling his joints pop. He sniffed; what was that burning smell?

"Can you smell that?" he said turning to Louise.

She was climbing to her feet, looking past Stan.

"Smells like something burning?" he said.

"It's time," said Louise and a cloud of smoke rolled out of her mouth with the words.

Stan stepped back from her, waving away the smoke.

"I'm sorry," she said.

"No ... you're a deathling."

"*He* made me do it. My mum ... she's a deathling too ... we both died in the same house fire. He said he'd destroy her soul if I didn't do as he said."

Spots of rain began to fall, stripping lines of flesh-coloured makeup from Louise's face to reveal charred skin beneath it. She lent forward and popped free contact lenses.

"I'm so sorry," she sobbed, looking at Stan with red eyes. Bloody tears ran down her cheeks.

*"Oh Stan Wisdom, you're so brave and handsome and I'm so pretty and young and a seer just like you. Please, please help me!"* The ugly falsetto voice came from the bottom of the hillock.

Stan knew who he'd see before he turned around. It was the *he* Louise had mentioned.

"Ta da!" said Sergeant Moses, laughing as he spread his arms wide. "Here he is, the amazing, vanishing Seer."

Lightning flashed and the three dagger handles in his chest winked like stars. Armbands were spread out in a circle around the hillock cutting off any escape route.

Louise stumbled down the incline towards him, her skin now just dark, peeling flesh. Smoke poured from her mouth. "I did it. Did what you said. You'll let her go now. You promised."

"I've already let her go. Now I'll let you go," said Sergeant Moses plucking a heartseeker from his chest and flinging it at Louise.

"No," shouted Stan, but there was nothing he could do.

Louise screamed as the dagger struck her in the chest. Stumbling, she turned to face Stan, hands clawing at the dagger, then was nothing but a ball of light, and then nothing. The dagger flew back through the air and slid back into the big deathling's chest.

"Have I broken your heart? Plenty more where she came from. I've had these lovelies all over the city. It's amazing how long a candle can hold her smoke when her mother's soul depends on it," said Sergeant Moses, laughing as he switched to the falsetto again. "*Monsters, monsters everywhere, Stan Wisdom, but I met this brave friendly monster called Gabby and she'll help us.*"

Stan clenched his fists. How could he have been so stupid?

Lightning flashed and a clap of thunder detonated directly overheard. It was so loud some of the armbands flinched.

"Stand your ground," growled Sergeant Moses as the rain started to pelt down.

Stan paced the hillock grinding his teeth. Louise had betrayed him, but she'd had no choice. She'd been caught in Sergeant Moses' grip just as he had. Now she was gone. He came full circle. The deathlings were spaced out all around the hill. His only option was to try to break out past the weakest link.

"No cars to torch this time, Seer," said Sergeant Moses. "Dead or alive the poster says. Your choice. Be sure of one thing: you ain't leaving here without me. You're surrounded, just like I was at Khartoum when I was with General Gordon and all the Mahdi's men, screaming and wailing, were climbing the walls. They plunged these magic daggers into me and I'll plunge them into you boy."

"Why are you doing this to me?" shouted Stan.

"You're evil made flesh. The Seer. The creature that cursed our beloved Death and caused him to fall into a never ending coma. The creature Death prophesied would be the doom of deathlings if he wasn't stopped."

157

"Liar!"

"What did you say, boy?"

"You're a liar. You put Death into the coma."

"Listen to him squirm and lie boys. Pitiful ain't it?"

In all his years fighting bullies Stan had learned one golden rule. If the fight was inevitable, and it often was with bullies, you had to strike first. Never hesitate, or your momentary advantage could be lost.

Stan turned and sprinted down the opposite side of the hill to Sergeant Moses.

"Stop him!"

Stan held out his arms for balance as his feet slipped on the rain-slick grass. If he fell, it was over. Ahead of him, three deathlings, a floater, a twig and a headless scattering, closed ranks.

"Let him through and I will rip every nerve from your body with my teeth," shouted Sergeant Moses as he stormed up the hillock.

*They're afraid of me*, thought Stan as he closed in on them. He could see it in their bloodshot eyes and the way their hands trembled. If they really believed Sergeant Moses' lies about him putting Death in a coma, they had to believe he had some sort of supernatural power. He pulled as terrifying a face as he could and screamed at them. It was enough to make them hesitate for a second.

As they belatedly lunged forward, Stan dived into a forward roll beneath them. Wet soil squelched against his back. He sprung to his feet and pelted towards the fairground.

Sergeant Moses appeared at the brow of the hill, roaring with frustration. Heartseekers were in the deathling's hands as he charged after Stan. When he reached level ground he'd be able to aim and throw. Stan had to reach the fairground and the shelter offered by the milling crowds.

He pumped his arms and legs, concentrated on the slippery ground. A hissing sounded behind him. He glanced over his shoulder. It was a heartseeker, cutting through the downpour towards him, blazing momentarily as lightning lit the sky.

Stan burst into the fairground and sprinted straight at the first stall he came to, sliding over the slick counter. Ignoring the carny's protests, he grabbed a dartboard and spun, holding it out in front of him. The heartseeker slammed into the board, knocking him backwards into the wall. The blade easily cut through the board, but it held firm against the hilt. The dagger point glistened an inch from Stan's chest.

"What do youz think youz doin'?" said the carny. All he could see was a young boy waving one of his dart boards around.

Stan threw the dartboard to the floor and jumped free of the stall, heading for the centre of the fairground.

"Aye, that's it, run and keep running ya little toe-rag," said the carny. As he reached down for the dartboard, it started to dance around, as the invisible dagger tried to yank itself free. He jumped up onto his counter and crossed himself.

"Jesus, saints and the Holy Mother protect me, me dartboard's possessed."

The deathlings were close behind, dodging though the crowd. Sergeant Moses was holding his other two heartseekers, waiting for his moment to strike.

Lightning forked down again, striking the stationary Ferris wheel. Lightbulbs burst releasing a shower of sparks and coloured glass onto the screaming crowd below. The Ferris wheel started to turn, its music warbling out of time. Carneys jumped free of stalls, rushing towards the malfunctioning equipment as the crowds rushed the other way blocking off the deathlings. Sergeant Moses pointed, ordering his troops in different directions.

Stan could see they were trying to outflank him. He snatched a couple of air rifles from a duck-hunt stall and dashed forward. The rain was hammering down now and he splashed through puddles. In the distance, sirens wailed.

A twig and a crumple appeared between two stalls. He levelled the air rifles and fired. As the deathlings flinched, he tossed away the rifles and jumped through the entrance of the *Hall o' Mirrors*.

Elongated, squat and stretched *Stans* crowded around him, all with rain-slick hair, sweaty faces, harried eyes and heaving chests. He wound deeper into the mirror maze, feeling the floor rock as somebody followed him in. Stan took a long breath and released it as quietly as he could. His pulse thudded in his head. The pursuing footsteps were close. A heartseeker, stretched then scrunched, rippled across mirrors hunting its target and suddenly accelerated. A mirror-Stan shattered, a hundred falling pieces reflecting a hundred heartseekers spinning in confusion.

"I see you boy," said Sergeant Moses, squat and wide-mouthed as a monstrous toad. His red tunic and gold buttons bulged and rippled as he stalked his prey. Stan grabbed a football sized shard of mirror and fled the reflection. A heartseeker rippled across the mirrors in pursuit and another mirror-Stan shattered.

Thin as a stick, with a bulging head, Sergeant Moses laughed as he stalked Stan on pipe-cleaner legs.

Stan burst out of the *Hall 'o Mirrors* and into the pounding rain, feet slipping from beneath him. He dropped the chunk of mirror. He snatched it up from a puddle, slicing a finger and blood dribbled down its surface. Ahead of him was the railway bridge that led out of the park.

"Give yourself up!" Sergeant Moses and his mob hurtled after him.

A stitch dug in Stan's side. He was short of breath. He knew that he couldn't keep going much longer. The rhythmic clatter of an approaching train mixed with the chaotic sounds coming from the fairground.

"I won't miss this time," said Sergeant Moses, lifting a heartseeker.

Stan ignored him, digging in for one last sprint, onto the bridge and then in one smooth motion, heart lurching into his mouth, he jumped over the railings and down onto the roof of the passing train.

Ridged metal smacked into his body. Winded, he slid sidewards across the slippery roof. He hung on with one hand as his legs peddled fresh air searching for a grip. Telegraph poles flashed by a metre behind his back. His toe found the top of a slender window frame. He pushed with his leg and pulled with his one-handed grip, rolling up onto the roof, gasping for breath.

A heartseeker arrowed towards him, parallel to the train roof, blade glistening with rain. Stan was still holding onto the chunk of mirror. With bloody fingers, he held it up, catching his reflection, waiting as the knife hissed through the rain, ever closer. The blade captured lightning. It was on him. A deadly blur. He spun the mirror away from the train.

The dagger twitched back and forth between Stan and his reflection in the mirror. Then, as if deciding that the reflection must be real as it was making a bid for freedom, it swooped down and smashed through the glass. It arced around heading back to the distant silhouette of Sergeant Moses on the bridge.

Stan gasped for breath and laughed. Laughed so much that he almost slid from the train's roof and this just made him laugh even harder. He'd escaped.

He lay back and let the train carry him further away from his pursuers. Rain pounded down onto his face. After a few minutes, the train slowed for a red signal at a set of points. He sat up and stared at a building in an industrial estate alongside the track. It was a huge red building and on the side was its name in letters ten feet high: *Lockups4U.*

It wasn't the name that snagged Stan's attention. He stood up. This wasn't coincidence, this was fate. The first letter of the name was a fat, cursive '*L*'. It was exactly the same font as his mum's *L* keyring. His mum had a lockup. This is where she had been coming each morning of the repeated day; a lockup. What did she keep in it? He was sure it could only be one thing: Secrets.

# 18

Stan clambered down from the train, dropping onto the gravel border alongside the track. Adults glowered at him through rain-streaked windows and opened-mouthed little kids pointed. The train driver leant out his window and shouting warnings but Stan was already heading into the industrial estate.

"I need the key for a lockup in the name Lucy Wisdom," said Stan, panting, when he reached Lockups4U's reception desk. "She's my mum. She sent me to collect something."

A muscly man, wearing a *Rippers Gym* T-shirt at least two sizes too small for him, sat behind the desk. He raised his head and looked skeptically at the boy before him: wild-eyed, dripping wet, battered and bruised with blood dripping from one hand.

"Is that right?" said the man. Veins and tendons stood proud in his bullish neck.

"She was coming herself, but she had to go to work. Emergency." Stan knew he didn't sound convincing, but in his rush to reach the lockup he hadn't been able to calm his mind enough to concoct a more plausible story.

The man stared at him. He had a pale, round pockmarked face that made Stan think of a golf ball. "Hop it, kid," said the man jerking a thumb towards the exit.

"I need to get into the lockup?"

"What's your mum's number," said the man picking up the phone. A huge bicep flexed, stretching the T-shirt to bursting point.

"She isn't home."

"Of course she isn't, she's at work," said the man. "What's her work number?"

"I can't remember."

"Mobile?"

"She doesn't have one."

The man looked down and tapped a keyboard. "If you're still here when I look up, I'm calling the police."

Outside, Stan kicked at gravel and cursed. He was so close to something, something important, he could sense it. He remembered his mum's words: *It's time for me to share some secrets with you now. It'll help you understand things. Hopefully, it'll make things easier for you.*

The giant *L* stared down at him, rain streaming from it like a waterfall.

He had to get the key. If he had the key, he could find some way to sneak past *golfball-head* and let himself into the lockup. He tried to visualise it. He was sure that there was a number stamped on the metal. That had to be the lockup number. He started to run.

He had to catch two different buses to cross the city. By the time he reached his neighbourhood the storm had moved on. He wiped clear a circle in the condensation covered windows. Deathling patrols were everywhere. He pulled up his hood and slumped lower in his seat watching them in his peripheral vision. They were on every corner, lookouts perched on roofs and scouts riding around atop vans and lorries. When cars stopped at junctions, deathlings carrying wanted posters stared in the windows checking for the Seer.

As the bus zipped along the high street, past the turn into his street, he glanced down towards his flat. The street was thick with deathlings. There was no way he'd make it to his flat without being seen, and even if he did, they'd be waiting for him inside. He stayed on the bus until it reached the end of its route.

He found a cafe and ordered a milkshake. It was powdery and sour, not a patch on Enzo's, and it sat congealing on the table as he tried to devise a plan. A nighttime raid? No, the deathlings would still be waiting and watching. The sewers? He could probably get close to the house, but he'd still have to emerge in the street. Driving a car through the front wall? This wasn't a video game.

A group of twigs drifted down the street and Stan twisted his body to face into the shop, chair legs squealing against the floor.

"You going to drink that or just sit there all day? There's other customers need that table," said the cafe owner, a slender man with a fleshy mouth peeking out of a bushy beard so wild it looked like one of Kalina's props.

Stan looked around. There was only one other table being used and no queue snaking down the street from the entrance. He sipped his milkshake. "It'd be a crime to rush a milkshake this good."

The owner grunted and went back to cleaning his counter.

Stan was on his feet. He slapped two pounds on the counter and ran out the shop, straight into the phone box outside. It was the man's beard that started the chain reaction of thoughts ... the fake beard, Louise's makeup, Kalina ... that led to the plan.

He dialled, listened to a ringing tone.

"Come on," he said.

The phone clicked and a voice said: "You have reached Doctor Razor's House of Hell, please leave your name, number and death wish after the tone."

"Kalina, it's me, Stan."

"Stan, there you are! I wondered where you were. There was nobody home when I called this morning."

"I'm sorry I haven't been in touch for a while," he said.

"Like, since yesterday," said Kalina, in her *Stan's-being-strange-voice*.

"Ah, yes ..."

"Are you doing that funny blinking?"

"What?"

"You know, eyelids up and down rapidly at inappropriate moments."

"No."

"You sure, Stan Wisdom?"

"Yes, look I need your help. Really need your help."

167

"Serious Stan, eh? Okay, whatever you need I'm here for you."

Stan looked at his watch. "Can you meet me at the bus stop outside the supermarket in half an hour?"

"Dobrze."

"I need you to bring something with you."

*

Stan waited in a charity shop across the road from the bus stop. Hidden behind mannequins wearing dresses and beads, with vases of daffodils at their feet, he could observe but not be observed.

Daffodil pollen tickled his nose and he sneezed.

"Bless you," said the old woman behind the counter.

When Stan looked up from blowing his nose, Kalina was standing by the bus stop with tool box in hand, just as she had promised. She looked around, tapped her foot and checked her watch.

Stan waited.

"Can I help you, dear?" asked the old woman.

"Just browsing," said Stan, without turning around.

"Okay, dear."

A bus pulled up obscuring his view of Kalina. Its side was covered by an advert for the *The Hourglass World ... the most amazing book you'll read this century!* People got on and people got off. The bus pulled away, kicking out fumes. Kalina waved a hand in front of her face and coughed. She checked her watch

168

again, looked up and down the street and muttered to herself. Stan was fifteen minutes late.

Still he waited. When he reached twenty minutes, he sighed. It was safe.

"Thank you," he said to the old woman.

"Not find anything you like, dear?"

"Too much to choose from."

She laughed, then stopped, mouth open, as Stan threw himself to the floor behind the mannequins.

"Oh dear, did you trip?" she said.

"Yes," said Stan peering between the mannequins legs. A large group of deathlings, led by Sergeant Moses had surrounded Kalina. The big deathling ordered them left and right to search shops. They must have listened into his phone call to her, followed her and then hidden, waiting for him to show himself.

"Is there a back way out of the shop?" Stan asked the old woman. "There're some bullies after me."

"Oh, how terrible. Follow me, dear." She led him through a curtain in the messy store room beyond.

Stan sprinted into the yard, out the gate and away.

"Come back tomorrow, we'll have new items," called the old woman, then she muttered to herself. "I should have offered him a cup of tea."

*

The next morning, Stan stole a mobile phone from a woman's handbag at a bus stop. Her husband chased him for a full five minutes. When Stan finally outran him, he bent over and gulped down air. He felt sick with nervous energy. He'd slept rough overnight, rather than risk being caught in somebody's house again, and he'd been bitten by ants. A track of red bumps ran up his neck to his cheek. His dyed blond hair resembled a crow's nest.

He stood staring at the phone. What he was about to do wasn't fair. He was going to put his only friend in mortal danger, but what choice did he have?

"Sorry Kalina," he said and dialled her number.

"It's me," said Stan, when she answered.

"Stan, there you are! I wondered where you were. There was nobody home when I called this morning."

"I was out scouting locations for a new film."

"A new film. You didn't tell me you had an idea for a new film. A secret, eh? *You know how much I love secrets, Mr Bond.*" The last sentence was said in her best North Korean villain's accent, which always sounded more like a Welsh accent.

"I've been keeping it under wraps. Until I was happy with it."

"Now you are?"

"Yep. You ready for a mystery tour of the story?"

"Imagine me clapping my hands with excitement and jumping up and down, that's your answer."

"Okay, keep your mobile with you. I'm going to give you clues about where to go."

"Clues?"

"Clues."

"Imagine even more excited clapping."

"First off, you need to get a bus into the city and visit the place where we laughed at the three-headed man."

"Don't need to be Mastermind to guess that one, it's ..."

"Don't say it," said Stan, too urgently, picturing unseen deathlings huddling around Kalina as he spoke. He sensed unease in the silence that followed.

"Everything okay?" she said.

"Absolutely," he said. "You up for this?"

"See you there."

*

The Museum of Contemporary Art (or, as Kalina liked to call it: The Museum of Splashes, Dashes and Dots) was housed in three interconnected warehouses in the centre of the city. Stan and Kalina often visited it in search of creepy ideas for their films. *Three-Headed Man*, a sculpture by the famous artist Maxwell P. Fandy had been exhibited there a year ago and the resemblance of the tortured heads to Mr Phillips, their maths teacher, possibly in the process of battling constipation, had reduced them to fits of uncontrollable laughter and led to them being walked off the premises by a security guard.

Stan watched Kalina arrive at the museum from the safety of a window seat in the cafe across the road. As he anticipated, she was being followed by Sergeant Moses and six deathlings. He dialled her number.

"Mr Bond?" she said.

"Quickly as you can, through the lobby and up the stairs to the top floor. Weave between people, act as if you are trying to lose invisible pursuers," he said as he watched her enter the building with the deathlings in close attendance.

"Will this be in the film?"

"Probably."

"Good, I like this. I'm on the way."

Stan could hear her Dr Martens boots squeaking as she crossed the lobby's marble floor. Her breath was loud in his ear.

*Please be safe, he thought. I'm so sorry for putting you in danger.*

He'd already been in the museum and worked out the route she'd have to take to have a chance of losing the deathlings.

Her breath rasped in and out as she dashed up the stairs.

"Lots of wobbly bowls and jugs with holes in here," said Kalina. "Not exciting me."

"Don't worry, the good stuff's on the way. Go straight through and turn left into the sculpture gallery."

"Shall I run? Might lose some pesky pursuers."

"Good idea."

Her breath rasped in and out and her boots squeaked rapidly as she ran. "Sorry. Oops! Underage pregnant girl coming through! Sorry. Only joking madam," she said.

Stan could imagine her weaving through the crowd. "Now, quick as you can, down the stairs and into the main exhibition space."

More rapid breathing and voices chattering in the background. Somebody laughed. Trainers squeaked and high heels clicked.

"Fog of the ... Forgotten Souls?" she said, catching her breath.

"Straight inside," said Stan.

Kalina took a deep breath and sighed. "Cool," she said, stretching out the word. The squeaking stopped. She was standing still. "As you know, Mr Bond, I abhor the overuse of the word cool, but this requires no lesser word. Have you seen this? The whole room's full of a coloured fog. There are lights shining from different directions so you pass though purple fog, then blue, pink, gold." She laughed. "I can barely see my hand in front of my face. You want to shoot a scene in here?"

"Something like that," said Stan.

"I mean, if you came in here with friends, unless you were holding hands, or standing close to them, you'd lose them."

*Exactly.* "Look down."

"Ah, that's how you find your way out. Discreet luminous markings. Different colours lead to different exits I presume. I'm liking this Mr Bond, I am liking this very much. As Uncle Andrzej used to say: When the woman gets off the wagon, horses have an easier time."

"What? Kalina, listen. I'm going to count down from three. When I get to zero, I want you to run as fast as you can out the room, following the red line. When you get outside jump on the number 114 bus, I'll be on it waiting for you. It's due in a few seconds," said Stan standing and leaving the cafe. There was the bus, just as it was yesterday when he checked.

"Like you can trust the bus timetable."

"This one's the same everyday."

"But ..."

"Three ..."

"... It's so cool in here."

"... Two ..."

"Okay, firing up engines."

"... One ... "

"I'm running!"

Stan sprinted across the road, flagging down the single-decker bus. For a moment, he didn't think the driver had seen him, but then the indicator blinked and he pulled over. Stan climbed aboard and faked searching for his cash.

"Hurry up, I haven't got all day," said the driver.

"Sorry," mumbled Stan, keeping his gaze fixed on the museum entrance as he turned out his pockets. Where was she? She should be out by now.

"Pay up or hop off," said the driver.

"Here it is," said Stan fishing coins from his back pocket as Kalina sprinted from the museum, tool box swinging in her right hand. Panting, she jumped aboard and Stan dumped two pound coins into the coin collector.

"Like that is it?" said the driver. "Okay, your girlfriend's onboard, now sit down."

The doors beeped closed as Sergeant Moses sprinted from the museum and chased the accelerating bus.

"That was cool," said Kalina, slumping down into a seat.

"Most definitely," said Stan. He watched Sergeant Moses recede into the distance and then sat by Kalina.

She hauled the tool box onto her lap and popped the lid open. "Now you can explain why I had to bring my monster make-up."

"I have a special commission for you," he said.

# 19

Two hours later, heart jerking like an animal in a trap, Stan stood at the top of his street. Deathling lookouts squatted on house roofs on both sides of the road. Others huddled around card games on car bonnets. There must have been at least thirty in total. He had to wait for the moment to make his move as he couldn't risk any humans being in the street. To them, he'd just look like a boy in monster make up. They'd stare at him and in an instant the deathlings would know he wasn't one of them. He'd already had to endure enough pointing, tutting and laughter as he headed back across town on a bus towards his neighbourhood.

Of course, Kalina had wanted to come with him.

"Stan Wisdom, you can't expect me to create such a masterpiece of makeup and then not tell me what it's for," she had said, applying texture to his grey skin with a stippling brush.

"I just want to try something out for the film."

"You are *such* a bad liar. If you're in trouble you know you can always ask for my help?"

"I've already asked more of you than I should." He grimaced as she inserted red contact lenses.

"You look like Uncle Radimir after a night drinking vodka with his old army cronies."

"That's exactly the look I was hoping for."

"You don't know Uncle Radimir."

"I can guess what he looks like."

Kalina grimaced and gave him one of her patented Kalina penetrating stares. "Us Eastern Europeans are closer to the old ways you know. We can sense things in the air. I think something is happening, something you're not telling me about."

For a giddy moment, Stan had considered telling her the truth. Sentences formed in his mind, but he knew this would only put her in even greater danger. Instead, he did something even more daring. He leant forward and quickly kissed her on the lips.

"Thank you," he said.

For once, Kalina had been lost for words.

He suppressed a smile at the memory as he shuffled forwards into his street. His face, neck and hands were pasty grey and clammy, mapped by prominent veins. His lips were morgue blue. Red contact lens scratched his eyeballs. His clothes had been swapped for some tatty old clothes that had belonged to one of Kalina's many cousins and a straggly black wig framed both sides of his face. Amazingly, it had only taken Kalina an hour to work her magic.

"They catch the Seer?" said a murder sitting on a garden wall. She had a long, bloodstained slash across her chest and cheeks swollen with bruises.

Stan shook his head.

The murder sucked her teeth and spat a dollop of blood on the floor. "Is the Sergeant coming back here?"

Stan raised his hands in a *your guess is as good as mine* way and shuffled towards his flat.

"I'm sick of this," said the murder wandering over to join a game of cards.

A huge, dreadlocked candle stood guard at the front door. One side of his face was charred and cracked with a sticky pit where his eye had been, the other side was undamaged. He held out an arm to block Stan's entry. His hand was a burnt stump. Smoke rolled from his mouth as he spoke: "Authorised personnel only."

"The Sergeant sent me to collect some keys," said Stan.

"Never said nothing to me before he left."

"He didn't know he needed them when he left. He knows he needs them now."

The candle shook his head. "Authorised personnel only."

Stan licked his lips, then cursed inwardly. He had to stop doing that or he'd lick away the makeup.

"Okay, if you don't want to let me in, fine, I understand, you're being cautious. When he comes back here yelling and shouting and fingering his heartseekers because he hasn't got the keys, I know who *I* will be pointing the finger at."

He pointed at himself and shook his head, then pointed at the candle and nodded. The candle half lowered his arm. Smoke curls twisted free of his nostrils.

"He's in a bad mood," said Stan, sitting down on the low garden wall, as if he was preparing to wait.

"Man, he's always in a bad mood."

"This is a really bad mood."

"Nothing new."

"If Mount Everest was a bad mood, that'd be his mood today."

The deathling curled his lip. "That bad?"

Stan nodded.

Sighing smoke, the candle stepped aside and waved him through. "Make it quick."

Stan climbed the stairs two at a time. The door to his flat was open. More deathlings were milling around inside looking at maps, ticking off streets on a long list.

"Sarge sent me for some keys," he muttered, raising his eyebrows into world-weary arches.

They nodded sympathetically and carried on with their checks.

In the kitchen, he was alone. He glanced over his shoulder and opened the little pot where his mum had hidden the key. It was empty. He opened the cupboard that held the key rack.

"No ... no ... no!"

The key hooks were empty.

He opened another cupboard to see if the keys had been moved there. They hadn't. He rifled though every shelf and started opening drawers. Cutlery and crockery clanked and rattled.

"Need any help?" shouted a deathling from the hall.

"I'm good," said Stan.

He checked under the sink, the window ledge, inside every cup and bowl, even the little ledge behind the boiler.

"No, we didn't, he got away! Because you lot are as much use as a fart in a suit of armour." The voice boomed up the stairs followed by the thud of boots. Stan could hear the deathlings on the landing scrambling to attention.

Sergeant Moses: The only exit from the kitchen was onto the landing. Stan wiped sweat from his brow and his fingers came away smeared with grey makeup.

"Welcome back Sarge," said one of the deathlings.

"*Sarge*? Did you just call me *Sarge*?"

"No Sergeant Moses ... I didn't say that Sergeant Moses."

"Good, my ears must have been playing tricks on me. Next time, you *didn't say that* I'm likely to rip off your head and use it as a bowling ball, if you get my drift"

"Your drift has mostly definitely been got, Sarge ... I mean ... aaaaggghh!"

The scream was followed by the sound of cracking bones and an uneven thumping. A head rolled into the kitchen, bouncing off a cupboard. It disappeared and a glowing sphere rose into the air and dissipated.

Stan kept his face pointing down as Sergeant Moses stormed into the kitchen with the other deathlings in pursuit. He was so tall his curly hair scraped the ceiling and his barrel chested bulk filled the space. The heartseeker hilts glittered.

"All they had to do was stay close to the girl and they lose her in the middle of some pink mist," said Sergeant Moses slamming a fist into the table. "Pink mist!" Cups danced and slowly rolled across the table, smashing on the kitchen floor.

"You, floater," said Sergeant Moses pointing at Stan. "Sweep that up. I don't want one of these idiots tripping up and accidentally slicing off a leg."

One of the murders tittered nervously. Sergeant Moses silenced him with a glare.

"What you waiting for?" said Sergeant Moses.

Stan's mouth was as dry as sandpaper as he saluted then grabbed the dustpan and brush. He could feel his make-up sliding down the side of his face.

Sergeant Moses turned his attention back to the others, barking out orders and stamping his feet. As Stan bent to sweep up the mess, he heard the jangle of keys. He glanced out the corner of his eye. All the house keys, including Lockups4U, were dangling from Sergeant Moses belt.

"I want the city divvying up between teams again. I want him! I want him found, now! If you can't find him, find the girl, the Polak. She was carrying a tool box. What were in it? We need to know what he's planning."

The *Polak*. Why had he dragged Kalina further into his war? After the kiss he'd told her not to go home for a couple of hours. She had to pretend she was on the run; it was all part of the story for the new film and they had to feel it to make it real. He hugged her tightly as she left, careful not to smudge his make-up.

"See you tomorrow."

*If tomorrow ever arrives.*

Sergeant Moses' booming voice dragged him back to the moment. "Any telephone calls? People calling at the house? Anything that might be a clue?"

The deathlings looked at each other and shook their heads as Stan poured the broken crockery into the waste bin.

Growling, Sergeant Moses pulled a heartseeker from his chest. Blood dripped from the blade. "This is my favourite dagger. It's made the most kills for me. It don't fall for no tricks and right now the poor thing's thirsty. It's dreaming of a bloody drink. If I don't see results from you sorry mob quick, I'll be letting it quench it's thirst on you. Now get out and find him." The last few words were shouted at a deafening volume and the deathlings scuttled from the room like leaves before a storm wind.

In the split second he realised he was about to be left alone with Sergeant Moses, Stan reacted. His grabbed a glass of water sitting on a worktop and filled his mouth, replacing it just as the deathling spun to face him.

"You! Out!"

Stan shuffled towards him, conscious of Sergeant Moses' eyes narrowing, suspicion crumpling his forehead. Sweat trickled down Stan's back and beaded on his forehead loosening his makeup.

Sergeant Moses held out a hand to block his path. His eyes narrowed. "Who are you anyway? I don't remember your ugly mug."

Stan's makeup felt like it could slide from his face, like a magician whipping a tablecloth from beneath a table full of crockery, at any second. He was paralysed by fear.

"Well? I asked a question," said Sergeant Moses stamping. The keys rattled on his belt.

The sound of his prize allowed Stan to force himself into motion. He opened his mouth as if to speak and water gushed between his lips. Sergeant Moses stepped back, face twisted in disgust.

"Floaters! I hate 'em. Don't know why Death saved any of you. Get out of here, leave me alone!" he said as Stan fussed, flapping his hands as if we was going to wipe down the Sergeant's tunic. "Leave it! Out!"

Stan saluted and headed down the stairs as quickly as he could without running. He opened his fist. The Lockups4U key was nestled in his palm. He'd managed to tug it free of Sergeant Moses' belt as the deathling tried to fend him off.

*Don't look back, whatever you do, don't look back*, he thought as he strode blinking into the sunlight and hurried towards the high street.

Deathlings glanced at him and then returned to waiting or gaming. They weren't interested in another deathling running errands for Sergeant Moses.

Stan allowed a smile to creep onto his face. He'd done it. He'd sneaked into the lion's den and stolen the key from beneath its paw.

The smile slid into a frown as the two youngest Collins brothers turned into the road, pushing and shoving each other as they fought over a bag of crisps. Carl tipped the bag into his mouth and blew a spray of crisp fragments into James' face.

James pushed him into the road, cursing as he wiped the soggy morsels from his cheeks.

They saw Stan before he could find shelter. Wicked grins creased their faces. James sniggered, elbowing his brother in the ribs and, slowly, Carl raised an arm and pointed.

"Oi! Psycho, sweet makeup? Trying to look like your gypo-girlfriend?"

Stan felt the weight of every deathlings' gaze fall on him.

# 20

The Collins brothers quickened their pace. Stan almost laughed at the absurdity of the situation. After everything he'd been through to get the key, these two idiots were going to be his undoing?

On both sides of the road, lookouts were sprinting over roof tops, jumping alleyways separating sets of terraced houses, pointing out Stan's position.

Behind Stan, Charlie jumped onto a car and stretched his mouth to fill his face. He cupped his hands around the hole and boomed out his alarm call.

*Ooohhhooowww!!!!!*

Deathlings spilled out of houses the length of the street. Sergeant Moses moved amongst them, bashing aside any that crossed his path. Fury lit his eyes when he saw who they were pursuing. He'd been tricked. The Seer had been within his grasp again and he'd let him slip free. He lengthened his stride into a road devouring run.

"We're going to teach you a lesson this time," said James Collins. They were only metres away.

Stan glanced at them, but he barely heard their words. He squeezed the lockup key until it bit into his hand, then fished his dad's lighter from his pocket. The only weapons he had to defend himself with: a key and a lighter. He spun to face the deathlings. Sergeant Moses was leading the mob. He could repeat his trick with a car's petrol tank, but this time the deathlings were all around him and he couldn't outrun them; not if he had to fight the Collins brothers first.

When Stan heard the van engine revving, he realised he had one more weapon: knowledge. He looked at his watch and started to run. With a screech of tyres, the white van with *Clean Me* written in the dirt on the side skidded around the corner and hurtled down the street scattering deathlings. The driver slowed momentarily, glancing at the boy dressed as a monster and gunned his engine again.

In the instant he slowed down, Stan sprinted into the road behind the van, jumped onto its back bumper and grabbed the door handle. The van's acceleration nearly yanked it free of his grip, but he clung on with all his strength as the Collins' brothers and Sergeant Moses sprinted down the street after him. At the end of the street the driver barely slowed, tyres squealing as he cornered, then raced onto the main road, his head swivelling, looking for clues on his endless quest for Paradise Street.

*

The afternoon storm was thundering its way towards the city when Stan arrived at Lockups4U. He'd changed back into his own clothes and scrubbed away the makeup. The huge L sign reflected a lightning flash. Thunder cracked as he entered the reception. The bald man with the pockmarked face, wearing the stretched-tight, *Rippers Gym* T-shirt sat behind the desk.

"Can I help you?" he said. Stan's less distressed appearance was enough to move the day away from their previous meeting.

"My mum sent me to collect something," Stan held up the lockup key with the *L* shaped fob. "Her name is Lucy Wisdom. Lockup number 136." The number was stamped on the key.

The man took the key from Stan and checked the number. He handed the key back, tapped at his computer, sighed and picked up the phone.

"What're you doing?" said Stan.

"Calling your mum."

"Why?"

"Computer notes. Says here nobody but her is allowed to enter the lockup. Seeing how she was here this morning, seems a bit strange she didn't take what she needed. I'll need to double check with her."

Stan could hear the dial tone. Six rings and then the answer phone kicked in. The deathlings would be listening.

"Don't ... it's a surprise for her," said Stan.

"A surprise." The man put the phone back on its cradle, nodding his head. "Of course it is. Do you have any ID to prove you're her son?"

Stan patted his pockets and shook his head. He knew how this was going to play out.

"Of course you don't." The man held out an arm. His bicep was as thick as Stan's leg. "Give me the key and I won't have to call the police."

Stan backed away, turned and ran. As he dashed into the car park thunder rolled across the sky and the heavens opened. The man dashed after him, but his bulky body couldn't keep up with Stan as he weaved between vehicles. Stan ducked out of sight behind a van. The man stood, muscles bulging, hands on hips, then tutted and ran back to the reception.

Stan knew he didn't have much time. He circled around to the back of the building and scrambled up an eight feet high, chain-link fence, topped with barbed wire. His trainers slipped on the wet wire. Thunder boomed again. It sounded like the end of the world. In the distance, lightning forked down. A swirl of wind delivered the sound of screams. The lightning had hit the Ferris wheel again. As he swung his leg over the barbed wire, the rain-filled wind tugged at his clothes unbalancing him and his jeans snagged on a barb.

"Come on," he shouted, leaning forward and trying to yank them free. He heard denim rip and the wire bit into his leg. He took a deep breath. The wind threw more rain into his face.

"One, two ... three ..." He hurled his body weight forward. This time he ripped the jeans free, but his momentum carried his leg over the fence, unbalancing him. Wire slipped though his fingers and he fell. He hit concrete and lay winded, looking up into the storm. When he stopped seeing stars, he grabbed the fence and hauled himself to his feet. Thankfully nothing was broken, but his thigh, visible beneath a torn flap of denim, was badly cut.

He limped up to the building and found a side door. Turning his face away, he smashed the glass with his elbow, and carefully reaching between shards of glass, slid back a bolt. He found himself in a low ceilinged corridor lined with metal beams just above his head height. At the end of the corridor was a T-junction. Here the ceiling rose up and he found himself among the lockups. They were bigger than he expected; each one had a roll-up garage door secured by a huge padlock. The number had been stencilled in the middle of each door.

Stan followed the number trail to his mum's lockup. As he approached, he heard a voice. He tiptoed forward and peered around the corner. The muscly man was already standing outside 136, changing the padlock. His head was bent to one side, pinning a mobile phone to his meaty shoulder as he spoke.

"This is a message for ... err ... Lucy Wisdom, from Jay at Lockups4U. I just wanted you to know that I think your lockup key's been stolen after you came here this morning. I've had some kid round here today claiming to be your son, trying to get access to your stuff. Don't worry, I didn't let him in. I've changed the padlock so your things are safe. Pop by when you're next in the area and I'll give you your new key." He hung up and slipped the phone and key into his pocket.

The clock was ticking again. Stan could imagine a circle of deathlings huddled around the answer phone in his flat. They

189

knew where he was now. Time was running out. Sergeant Moses would be on the way.

"You can't stop me that easily," said Stan stepping into the corridor.

"You little toe-rag."

Stan ducked back around the corner and the man sprinted after him. "I'm gonna call the police you know."

Stan retraced his steps, running as fast as his limp allowed. Left, right, left and he was back in the corridor with low beams. It must have been a while since the man had been in the corridor, or in his haste to catch Stan, he may have forgotten how low the ceiling was. When his bald forehead whacked into one of the beams a gonging sound echoed down the corridor and he collapsed, unconscious onto the floor. A bump was already rising on his forehead. Stan took his mobile phone and the key for 136 and ran back to the lockup.

He took the padlock in one hand. Held the key in the other. The key felt ice cold. He hesitated. Everything that had happened to him since he revealed himself to the deathlings had been leading him here, but now he found himself unable to enter. He had no idea what he would find inside and that terrified him.

Thunder boomed, breaking his paralysis. The padlock clicked open and he grasped the handle. The door jerked upwards on rusty rollers and then stuck. Stan pulled again but it refused to move. Holding his breath he crouched down on his hands and knees and crawled inside as thunder rattled the building's bones. He pulled the door closed, plunging himself into darkness.

There was a noise behind. Something moving in the lockup. *Somebody* moving?

"Who is it?"

No answer.

He jumped to his feet. There had to be a light switch. He slapped the walls. He couldn't find a switch. His pulse pounded in his ears. He'd forgotten to start breathing again. Stars spangled in the darkness. With trembling fingers he flicked his dad's lighter into life. A figure stared back at him from the corner of the room. Staggering backwards he fumbled the lighter and plunged back into darkness.

# 21

Backing away until he bumped into the wall, Stan flicked the lighter to life again and held it at arm's length to illuminate the figure.

"Idiot." There was nobody there; just a ghost conjured by angles, flickering shadows and an exhausted mind.

He turned around and patted the wall until he found a light switch. A strip light flickered into life and he pocketed the lighter.

The lockup was empty except for an ornate, wooden box, the size of a shoebox, sitting in the middle of the floor. Stan circled it. The hinged lid was inlaid with a checkered pattern made from different types of wood and polished to a high sheen. The brass hinges were fashioned as Arabesque swirls. It looked like an expensive antique.

Stan sat down, cross-legged in front of it. He took the lid in his hands. The wood was cool and smooth. *Open it*, his mind said, but his body didn't respond. His hands felt like they belonged to somebody else. His breath came quickly, his heart raced.

Why would his mum hide away this box, unless it contained something that she didn't want him to see? Something she had to keep, but didn't want to risk him seeing? He sat immobile. Hands on the lid.

Thunder shook the building again. Stan flipped the lid open. A layer of jewellery glittered in the harsh light like a mini pirates' hoard. Stan dipped in a hand: a feather light pendant holding a teardrop-shaped ruby; rings encrusted with diamonds; swirling broaches encrusted with a rainbow of precious stones. These had to be worth thousands of pounds. Why hadn't his mum sold them rather than scrape by on her wages?

He dug down into the box, clearing away the jewellery. There had to be something else. At the bottom of the box were two more items. A pen and a leather bound journal embossed with the initials LSM. He opened the journal. On the inside cover, beneath the printed message THIS DIARY BELONGS TO somebody had written:

Louise Stefanie Mather.

Stan looked at the cover again. Flipped back to the inscription. It didn't make sense. He knew the handwriting; it was his mum's. Who was Louise Stefanie Mather?

There was only one way to decipher the mystery, that was to read on:

*1st November*

*What a day, Journal! What a day! I used to dream about days like this when I was scribbling away in my little attic flat. I used to tell myself: Louise girl, one day you'll finish this book, you'll show it to an agent and they'll love it. They'll show it to lots of publishers and they'll love it even more and pay you lots of money for the privilege of selling it to the public. You'll have a wonderful launch party with everybody telling you how wonderful you are (while they force you to drink champagne and eat nibbles shaped like little swans). And to top it off you'll meet the man of your dreams - the archetypal tall dark mysterious man (let's use TDMM for short). Well, I had to write three novels before an agent took a shine to one - All The Dead Things. But here I am! I sold a novel - for lots of money - I can do what I always wanted to do and become a full time writer. And there was a TDMM at the book launch. And I think he likes me!!!! He's called Marcus Quint - strange name, fantastic smile and ... I asked him why he was at the book launch and he said he just liked the title of the book. I just kept looking at his smile, his dark mysterious eyes, broad shoulders .... time for bed. I've had too much champagne, I might write something smutty.*

Could this really be his mum's handwriting? It looked like it, but the words were light and full of fun and the story bore no resemblance to her life. She'd never mentioned anything about being a writer and he'd certainly never heard of a Marcus Quint.

*31st December*

*My New Years Resolution: I MUST WORK HARDER ON MY NEW BOOK and spend less time with TDMM! My agent has been telling me off again ... don't waste your momentum ... blah, blah, blah, ... stay in the public eye ... la, la la ... But it's so hard to do when TDMM whisks you off to Paris for the weekend or the*

194

*Maldives for a week. One thing I have learnt: sand between the toes begets feathers between the ears! He treats me so well. And he really TREATS me. Yesterday he bought me a ruby necklace - its heartbreakingly beautiful. Rings, bracelets - I feel like Cleopatra. I said that to him and he joked that he'd met her once. I only wish he wasn't so secretive. I'm ready to move on from the tall, dark, MYSTERIOUS man stage to the tall, dark, GETTING TO KNOW YOU VERY WELL man. A girlfriend asked me what his job was last week and I really couldn't answer. Whenever I ask him he gives me these long rambling answers that seem to make sense at the time but are nonsense when I try and tell anybody else. And he does have this annoying habit of being able to move soundlessly around the flat. I'll be standing in the kitchen, pouring a glass of wine and suddenly he'll be at my shoulder. He always laughs when I jump ... it's the one little thing that really irritates me. Anyway, who cares. That smile! Those eyes! A very unexpected thought popped into my mind today - dare I write it down? Go on Louise girl, it's what journals are for!!!! - today I thought: I could have babies with this man. How Scary-Mary-from-the-dairy is that!!!*

The lockup's door rattled as a gust of wind hurtled down the corridor. The strip light buzzed. Sergeant Moses was on the way. He should take the journal and run. Read it later. He couldn't stop. He flicked forward.

*5th January*

*Okay, didn't expect that. Didn't expect that at all. I've been thinking about saying the words to him for weeks. Maybe a month. Just looked back through the journal and it is exactly a month. I thought he'd like it - maybe even love it. I thought it'd show him how much I loved him. They were big, scary life changing words and they took a lot to get out. Three (big) glasses of wine before I said them: one day I'd like to have babies with you I said.*

*His face changed. Went flat. Blank. He moved close to me. Towered over me. I thought he was going to hit me.*

*Never, ever speak of this again, he said.*

*I swear the room went dark and he seemed to fill the space.*

*I won't speak of it again. Because I won't ever be seeing him again. I'm not going down that route. My dad used to hit my mum. I have a life. I have my dignity. I'm not going down that route.*

Nausea wormed its way into Stan's stomach. He was gripped by a desire to stop reading; to set the journal aside and run, but he couldn't.

*28th Feb*

*The new novel is complete. I don't like it. It's sour and gloomy. My agent hummed her appreciation and suggested some changes: she suggested <u>lots</u> of changes and ......*

*Journal, I'm not being honest with you......*

*I'm wittering on about the book when I should be setting down my other news. Truth is I'm scared about how you'll take it. I know I swore I wouldn't see TDMM again after the last time. But*

196

*I have. There ... I said it. Marcus is back. He begged my forgiveness. Apologised. Apologised so deeply. He's explained himself too. Explained how an old girlfriend tried to trap him in a relationship by getting pregnant. He doesn't want children. But he wants me. He is being 100% honest with me. I can feel it. I believe him. I honestly do. I think he can make me happy journal.*

Stan turned the page. Wind howled around the building mixing with another noise that grew louder by the second: *Ooohhhooowww!!!!!*

*15th March*

*Why won't he share himself with me? Why won't he tell me what he does, where he goes? Is he a gangster? Is he a spy? An astronaut? Does he work at Mcdonalds, Euro Disney, down a coal mine, up a crane ... aaaggghhh!!!! He could be anything. And how does he do that popping up out of nowhere thing???!!!*

*He's done it again!!! I can hear him moving around in the living room, but the front door **did not** open!! It's squeaky. I'd hear it. That's starting to spook me.*

*Who is he?*

*1 April*

*I caught Marcus talking to himself today. When I say talking to himself, I mean talking to fresh air. As if there was somebody standing in front of him when there plainly wasn't. He was talking* *about <u>SOULS</u>. Yes journal ... I said .... <u>SOULS</u>. I asked him if it was an April's Fool - he looked at me with that sorry blank face he does. You shouldn't have heard that, he said to me. Then laughed and used his smile. It didn't work this time, but I didn't let on. He didn't mention it again, but he was off with me all night and he disappeared about 11pm.*

*12th April*

*I'm pregnant. Oh, God help me ... journal ... I'm pregnant.*

*15th April*

*I told him. I expected the blank face. Or a rage. Instead, he smiled sadly and stroked my face. Kissed me. A child, he said, what a sweet dream.*

*I told him it wasn't a dream. It was real. We're going to have a baby.*

*I can't, he said.*

*Yes you can, I said ....and then ... I swear this is true journal. Mad as it seems as I sit here and write these words.*

*He disappeared.*

*One second he was in front of me, the next he was gone.*

*I am Death, he said. He was standing behind me.*

*I turned around.*

*I'm sorry, he said. And disappeared again. He reappeared by the front door. In your heart you've always known I was something else, haven't you.*

*I nodded at him. I didn't have any words. What can you say when you are presented with undeniable evidence of the supernatural? Somehow I found some words for my baby.*

*I don't care what you are, I told him. I could feel a warmth spreading through me. It was the warmth of truth, of certainty, of love. You love me and you'll love this child. I know you will, I said to him.*

*He hesitated. Smiled. Said: Could I, really?*

*Yes, I said.*

*If only this had happened a year ago, he said. I might have been strong enough to hold him off. Now, I'm not sure ... He shook his head and smiled that sad smile again.*

*Hold who off? I said.*

*The cuckoo in my nest. My right hand and my doom.*

*I don't understand, I said.*

*Then he fixed me with a stare as heavy as stones. If I don't return - run. Run and don't stop running because he won't let you or the baby live.*

*Who? I said, but he disappeared and all he left behind was fear.*

*17th April*

*HE came. Red tunic. Red eyes. Daggers in his chest. He appeared out of nowhere. I dropped a jar of tomato sauce and it splashed up white cupboards like blood. He stomped up to me, pinning me against the wall with his presence. His skin was grey and his breath smelt of liver.*

*He doesn't ever want to see you again, he said, his face so close.*

*And the baby has to die. Tomorrow, you go to the clinic and get it done, or I will see it done with my heartseekers. He stroked his dagger hilts. I am Sergeant Moses, his right hand. His voice.*

*I swear I don't know where I got the courage from - it must have come from my baby. But I stared back into his red eyes and told him he was a liar. I told him he was nothing but a cuckoo in the nest. I closed my eyes, waiting for the knives to strike. He just laughed.*

*Spirited. I like that in a woman, he said. I will return tomorrow. The baby will be dead when I get here.*

*He vanished.*

*I slid to the floor amongst the broken glass and clutched my belly.*

*What am I to do? What's happened to Marcus? Where is he?*

*18th April*

*Fear drove me to the clinic, but love saved my baby. I couldn't do it. They said I was going to have a little boy and suddenly I could imagine what he'd feel like in my arms. What his head would smell like - that warm, milky baby smell. I've held my friends' babies. I want to hold my own. I want to have my baby. I made a decision there and then.*

*I'm going to do as Marcus said. I'm going to run. I'm going to run, hard and fast and not stop. If Moses and his supernatural allies come after me - so be it. I'm a writer. I'm inventive. I'll rewrite myself. Create a new character.*

200

*This is the last entry I will write as Louise Stefanie Mather. From now on, I'm going to be become Lucy Wisdom. I'm going to leave my old life behind: my career as a writer, my money, my friends and family. I'll change my appearance. Lose weight. Change my hair colour. Start wearing glasses. I won't stay anywhere for too long.*

*I want my baby boy. I won't give in to fear.*
*I want my baby boy.*
*I'm going to call him Stan.*


"No!" Stan's mind spun, images flickering like an old film. *My dad died when I was three. In the supermarket. I saw it. He was my dad.* But a voice in his head said: *lies. Lies designed to keep you safe.*

"No, no, no ..."

His fingers fumbled as he flipped through random entries.


*I'm free of him journal. I'm Lucy Wisdom now. I look like a different woman. I have a baby boy ... STAN! xxxx But I <u>MUST</u> be careful. I know Moses' invisible helpers are out there. I can't see them, but I can sense them. It must be all the time I spent with Marcus. I'll be walking down the street and I'll just know one is nearby. I get goosebumps all over me. Hairs on the back of my neck like antennae!!*


*Stan said his first word today - Mummy! I cried. He smiled. Precious boy, I will never let anything happen to you.*

Stan scrambled through the journal, skipping pages, flying through the years.

*I've met a man. A good man. His name is Charlie. If it works out between us, I'm going to tell Stan he's his dad. I HAVE TO PROTECT HIM FROM THE TRUTH.*

*They took him! I was in the supermarket. I knew one of them was near. One of HIS helpers. I could sense it. And oh my dear God ... Stan could SEE it. He could actually SEE it ... he called it a monster. The doctors said Charlie died of a heart attack. Maybe it was, maybe it wasn't. But they were involved. And they'll know Stan can see them ... how do I protect him now????*

*The counsellor is working ... anyway, I think she's working. I have to make Stan think these monsters are in his head. I have to make him ignore them. It's the only way he'll ever be safe. I can't sense them anymore. Too long away from Marcus. But I know they're out there.*

*Journal. I'm moving you to a lockup. Stan's getting too curious about things. Fingers in every pie, cupboard, drawer. You name it, he's in it. He's a good reader. Bright boy. Time to hide you away from prying eyes.*

"No!" said Stan standing, dropping the journal as the lockup spun around him. Three photos skidded across the floor. "No!"

All logic said: Yes. The journal was a missing piece in a puzzle. Now all his mum's more eccentric behaviour made total sense. It was all to protect him. How could she lie about *this* ... how could she not tell him!

*My father is Death, that is why I can see deathlings. That's why I'm the Seer.*

Thunder crashed outside and this time he heard Charlie's deathling siren.

He picked up the photos. The first one was his mum sitting behind a table at her book launch. Piles of books sat at each end of the table and she had one open in front of her, scribbling her autograph inside. The second photograph was of Stan as a newborn baby.

The third was his mum standing arm in arm with a man on a wide lawn before some stately home. He was tall, over six feet with dark hair neatly combed into a side parting. He was handsome and his smile raised his good looks to another level.

Death - his father.

Stan leant closer, trying to drink in as much detail as he could. The lockup dropped out of focus. All he saw was the picture. He felt as if he was standing on the edge of it. He could smell the grass and feel the warm breeze on his cheeks. The man slipped his arm from his mum's and started to move towards Stan. At first he walked forward, stride lengthening, then he was running, sprinting, filling the picture blotting out the scene.

"No!" yelled Stan dropping the photograph as an arm thrust free of it, the edge of the picture stretching around a bicep, but

203

refusing to open further. The arm thrashed around, palm slapping the floor, fingers flexing, *reaching for him.*

Then he heard the voice: "Come to me, my son ... please come to me."

Stan ran.

# PART THREE

# DEATH

## 22

The wind whipped rain into Stan's face as he sprinted into the car park. Lightning danced across car windows and thunder set off car alarms. Overhead, power lines rocked and sang. Charlie's siren call throbbed through the air.

*The arm stretching the picture frame.*

*Mum, why didn't you tell me? I could have helped. I could have saved you. I could have ...*

The thought snapped off as somebody called his name. Was Death following him? Somehow, Stan was stumbling along the railway lines, a steep embankment on one side. He couldn't remember leaving the industrial estate. He slowed as an ankle twisted on the chunky stone ballast. He hopped up onto the rails but they were too slippery to walk on.

"Stan!"

This time he heard the voice clearly. He glanced over his shoulder. It was Gabby, her hair plastered to her ruined face, body rocking awkwardly as she ran along the railway line after him.

"Please, wait."

Stan ignored her, leaning forward into the storm, lungs burning. He wanted to leave them all behind. He didn't want this new life.

"... Ser ... Moses ... all of them ...." Gabby's sentence was ripped up and scattered by the storm.

Moses - the name was a hook. Stan glanced over his shoulder again and lost his balance. His right foot shot sidewards sending gravel clattering down the embankment. He tried to correct his balance, but his stance was all wrong. He pitched forward bouncing and rolling down the slope. Gravel bit his back and smacked his skull as a mini-avalanche clattered down with him. He came to rest against the litter-strewn line of trees, nettles and thorn bushes flanking the train line. He pushed himself to his feet using an abandoned shopping trolley.

"You okay?" Gabby was sliding down the slope.

"Leave me alone." Stan pushed his way through the trees. He was limping heavily.

"Stan please."

"It's all true!" he shouted, rounding on her.

Surprised by his anger, Gabby stumbled and fell backwards onto the embankment.

"I don't want to be ... this. I don't want to be like you!"

"Listen to me," she said. "You have to calm down and follow me. They're coming ..."

"Let them come. I'm going to ..."

"What are you going to do? Eh? You want to beat Moses? We can do that, but we have to get away from here first."

"I ..." Words deserted him.

"I understand," said Gabby, climbing to her feet.

"No, you don't," said Stan, but the violence had left his voice.

More voices carried to them on the wind. "We have to go. Now."

She set off through the trees. Stan limped after her. His anger had been replaced by a profound exhaustion, as if all his rage had detonated in one huge explosion and all that remained was the smoking ruins of his mind and body.

The pursuing voices were closing in; groups of deathlings calling back and forth. Gabby and Stan entered the industrial estate. Huge puddles danced under the storm's assault. Gabby led him to the nearest building, a featureless grey warehouse. A sign above its doors read: *Torso Town*.

Its big sliding doors were partially open and they slipped inside. The rain hammered down on the corrugated iron roof thirty feet overhead. It was a relief to be free of its incessant pummelling. Stan scooped water from his eyes. The warehouse's ground floor was full of mannequins, some adult sized, others child sized. Most were covered head to toe by opaque plastic bags and arrayed in ranks as neat as the Terracotta Warriors. There was no sign of any staff except for one security guard in a small room just off a balcony on the first floor. He was facing away from the window, earbuds in, feet up and tapping in time to music, as he read a newspaper.

"In here! Check every flipping warehouse!" The deathlings were outside.

Stan stood frozen, staring at the doors, waiting for them to enter.

"Shift it." Gabby grabbed a couple of the bags and started to weave in amongst the dummies. Stan followed.

"Over your head. Still as a statue until they're gone."

Stan did as she said, raising the bag over his head and wriggling his way into it. It was stiflingly hot inside and in seconds he could feel his damp clothes steaming. Sweat ran down his brow and slid, stinging into his eyes.

"I'm not checking all these, we'll be here for hours," said a deathling.

"You do as you're told," said another.

Footsteps echoed across the warehouse and plastic bags crinkled as the deathlings started to check.

"Nice legs."

"Nicer than yours."

"Maybe, but this one's got more between its plastic ears than you've got between your maggot eaten ones."

"Yeah?"

"Yeah!"

"Less banter and more searching."

There were three of them. Stan could see their blurred outlines moving closer. Stopping, bending, lifting the plastic coverings. He tried to breathe as quietly as he could, but the air was tropical within the plastic. Sweat covered his face and ran down his back and sides. Condensation beaded the inside of the bag. The deathlings would see it. Where was Gabby? A deathling bent to inspect the mannequin in front of him, muttering. Stan could smell smoke. It was a candle.

"Waste of time," said the deathling straightening up. Stan could hear its ligaments popping. Its dark, charred face was no more than three feet from his, but all it could see was a plastic bag covering a child shaped dummy. Stan willed himself to hold steady. He held his breath so as not to disturb the plastic close to his mouth.

The deathling took a step closer. Its silhouette was clear through the bag. It bent down and grabbed the plastic. It crackled as it rolled the plastic upwards exposing Stan's feet.

# 23

"Quick, get down here. I've got an idea," shouted a deathling from the front of the warehouse.

"One more," said the deathling, rolling the plastic higher.

Stan's lungs were starting to burn. He was desperate to breathe.

"No more. Here now!"

"All right, keep your hair on. Oh sorry, I forgot you don't have a head to keep any hair on," said the deathling, laughing and spewing out clouds of smoke as he dropped the plastic.

Stan gulped smoky air and willed himself not to cough. He could hear the deathlings talking; a brief discussion and then burst of cackling. They shouted out a countdown together: "Three ... two ... one!"

The thud and crackle of falling plastic-wrapped mannequins filled the warehouse. The deathlings hooted and hollered. Stan's heart lurched as the plastic wave swept towards him. The deathlings were toppling the mannequins like carefully arranged dominoes. Instinctively, he stiffened his body. As the mannequin in front fell into him, he rocked back, sending the mannequin behind him into the next one. He landed amongst a tangle of limbs with plastic feet digging into his back. He lay still as the noise moved away from him and then ended.

"Nothing here but plastic," said one of the deathlings.

"Wait a second. See if anything moves," said another.

Stan's back was agony, his lungs on fire, but he lay still as the Deathlings surveyed the warehouse.

"Come on," said another. "Nothing here."

"Okay, let's go."

"That was fun," said the final one. "Can we find more dummies?"

"You are one, and …"

When Stan heard them leave the warehouse he ripped himself free of the plastic, coughing as he filled his lungs with clean air.

"What the ... what have you done?" The security guard was standing on the first floor balcony looking down onto the mess below. He pulled a mobile from his pocket. "You stay just where you are, Sonny Jim. The boys in blue will be here in a mo' and they'll be wanting to have a word with you."

Stan watched Gabby wrestle her way out from her plastic bag and then looked up at the security guard. He'd put the phone to his ear, but now his hand was slowly descending as if the phone had become as heavy as a dumbbell. His mouth fell open. All he could see was one of the plastic bags moving on its own.

Gabby glanced at Stan and then dashed across the warehouse towards the stairs, moving the plastic bag though the

212

air like a ghost. She used her fingers to make a wailing mouth in the front of the bag.

The security guard crossed himself and mouthed *Oh My God!* He fumbled his phone and it tumbled through the air, smashing into pieces on the warehouse floor. He didn't care. He was already dashing down the opposite set of stairs. When he reached the ground floor, he looked over his shoulder at the ghost one last time and then sprinted out into the storm.

Gabby rocked up to Stan.

He jabbed a finger at her. "No more secrets. You tell me everything now."

"Let's get out of sight," she said.

The security guard's office was furnished with a couple of chairs, a table and a radio. A bank of monitors showed the warehouse, inside and out, from every angle and they watched deathlings in the car park, searching industrial dustbins and checking under cars.

There was a little fridge in the corner of the room containing egg sandwiches, cans of coke and bananas. Stan realised he was famished. They sat in silence as he ate. When he'd finished, he felt his eyes sagging. He tried to fight it, but his body was exhausted. Sleep took him.

It was dark outside when he opened his eyes.

"Better?" said Gabby.

"You should have woken me."

"You're going to need all your strength. Best that you rested."

Stan yawned and stretched.

"What you was saying about no secrets? I've been thinking about that," said Gabby.

"Good."

"I want to tell you what it was like when I died. When I became a deathling. It'll help you understand who we are."

"Okay."

Gabby took a deep breath. "When I died. When *we* died, me and my bruvver. We were just too young. We didn't know nuffink about nuffink. One minute we were alive, the next we were gone. Just like that." She clicked her fingers.

"We were getting crushed and then suddenly we were light. We were light and somebody was holding us in their hands. It was a deathling, but I didn't know that did I. All I could concentrate on was the light."

She took another deep breath and continued.

"I was terrified. Floating before this great big white light, feeling myself drifting apart. I reached out for Joe, but I couldn't find his hand. I didn't even have a hand to find it with. I was breaking up and already I didn't feel like me. I haven't got the words for explaining how it was. Just think of the most scared you have ever been and then multiply that by the number of grains of sand you find on the beach and that isn't close."

Her face crumpled as she stroked her half-coin pendant. Stan could feel its other half, heavy in his pocket, and he fought an urge to place his hand over it, as if it needed hiding.

Gabby shook her head dislodging bloody tears and kissed the pendant. She took a deep shuddering breath.

214

"Then he showed up: Death. Out of nowhere. Suddenly I had a body again. Joe was standing by me. I can't remember what Death said anymore. His words were like poetry ... like medicine. He was telling us how he understood our fear. It was okay to be afraid. We weren't the first and we weren't gonna be the last who couldn't cross. There was a role for us. A noble role. We could help people, help souls just like us get safely to Forever. We could become deathlings, but we had to be sure of our choice because once it was made we'd never be able to cross, and we'd have to live with the pain of our death for ever. At that moment, that seemed like a small price to pay to avoid the terror of the unknown. So we agreed and we became deathlings."

"How does it work? How do you know when somebody is going to die?" said Stan.

"Death can read the Universe, or somefink like that. Anyhow, he just knows and then the order comes down: *Gabby, you be at such-and-such a place at such-and-such a time.* Sure as eggs is eggs the person would die. Then we'd save their soul and make sure it went on its way to Forever."

"You keep saying that. What is it?"

Gabby shrugged. "Forever? That's too much of a high-fallutin question for me. All I know is that it's what comes after now."

Stan held up a hand, whispering. "Did you hear that?"

"What?"

"Sounded like somebody moving around down there."

He crept out onto the balcony and peered down into the warehouse below. The dummies still lay higgledy-piggledy across the floor. He couldn't see anybody. He held his breath and listened. The storm had stopped now and there was no sound other than the distant clatter of a passing train and water dripping from the roof. He returned to the office.

"Anyfink?"

"Can't see anything." He studied the security screens, but they all showed grainy, grey scenes devoid of people, or deathlings.

He sat down again. "So what now?"

"While you were in the safe house, I met with Herne in secret. He's found out where Moses is holding Death. I'm waiting on a message from him, then we meet with what's left of the resistance and we make our move."

"What am I supposed to do?"

"Herne says you can wake Death."

"How?"

"You're his son. You'll find a way."

"I'm glad you've got so much faith in me."

"Tomorrow's the day we've been waiting thirteen years for. We take down Moses. We start time again. We put your father back in charge."

"Death's son." Stan shook his head. "I just can't … I don't …"

"I know it must be difficult for you, but it's really an amazing thing. When humans talk about Death, they think of something bad, this monster in a black cloak with a big scythe stealing lives. It ain't like that. Death's a hero. He saves souls. You're going to be the same."

216

"And my mum?"

"She's alive. Herne saw her yesterday."

Relief washed through Stan, but it was tinged with anger. Even though his mum had acted out of love, keeping secrets to protect him, he couldn't forgive her. All those years seeing Joan, trying to persuade him that the monsters didn't exist. Why hadn't she prepared him for this? Why hadn't she told him who his true father was?

"Can't say the same about Joe," said Gabby. "Still no sign of him. I've got to hope that Moses is keeping him captive too."

She lapsed into silence, then said, "What's the matter?"

"What do you mean?"

"You look like you've swallowed a handful of needles," she said.

A confession rose to Stan's lips. He opened his mouth, hesitated, then swallowed it. It wasn't the right time. He would tell her what happened, but not now.

Not now.

"I was thinking about my mum," he said.

Gabby nodded. "Moses has hurt people we both love and we're going to make him pay."

The door slammed open and Stan scrabbled to his feet.

"Having a good time are you?" It was the security guard. His eyes were red and his breath stank of beer. "What you on? Glue? Dope? Something stronger? I'm not going to fall for your stupid ghost tricks this time. I'm not scared of trash like you."

Stan held up his hands. "Don't worry. I'm leaving."

"I don't think so. You aren't safe to be out on the street. I heard you talking to yourself. Death's son are you? Ha - sounds like you're messed up to me. Maybe one of them druggies that's into devil worship I read about in The Sun."

Stan stepped forward. "Listen all ..."

"Not so quick," said the guard. Suddenly he had a pair of handcuffs in shaking hands.

Gabby moved alongside the guard.

"Gabby, no," said Stan.

"He's going to 'cuff you."

"It's okay."

The guard looked back and forth between Stan and the fresh air he was talking to. "You really do need a night in the cells to straighten you out."

Gabby moved close to the guard, raising her hands to his back.

"No," said Stan. "Look at the time."

Gabby glanced at the clock in the corner of the office and nodded.

"The old *get-him-to-look-at-the-clock-and-make-a-run-for-it-trick*. I wasn't born yesterday, you know," said the guard, as a massive yawn seized him.

"Five ... four ... three ..." counted down Stan.

"Button it, sonny." The guard's eyes started to close. Another yawn split his face.

"Two ... one ..."

The guard vanished and reappeared sitting in his chair, arms folded with his feet on the desk. Rattling snores shook his chest.

"Midnight," said Gabby.

A snatch of music rang out and Gabby fished an iPhone from her smock pocket.

"What?" she said catching Stan's expression. "You don't think deathlings use phones."

She stroked the screen and smiled as she read a message. She showed it to Stan.

2MORROW THE TUNNELS

"We're on," she said.

# 24

Before the guard woke the following morning, Stan and Gabby headed into the heart of the city. It was the maddest rush hour Stan had ever seen. Endless streams of vehicles crowded the streets, engines growling as they inched forwards. Sweat beaded foreheads and soaked clothes. Radios blared out bad news. Angry flesh pressed against glass. Horns blasted, curses flew and tight fists were shaken.

Traffic lights cycled endlessly - red, amber, green, red amber, green - slicing traffic into chunks. Steam burst from overheated engines. A man chewed on his steering wheel. Another jumped from his car, abandoning it at a set of faulty traffic lights and a storm of horns rose from the vehicles trapped behind.

Commuters flooded the pavements, merging at junctions, weaving around each other, faces taught with anxiety. It was too hot for commuting. Men loosened ties and wrestled free of their jackets. Women fanned themselves with newspapers. A couple of men bumped into each other and a fight broke out.

On some unconscious level people were becoming *aware* of the repeated day. They knew something was wrong; something beyond their comprehension. Fear gnawed on their nerves. Stan felt it vibrating through his body. He rubbed his temples to try to ease the pressure,

"Are you okay?" said Gabby.

Stan shook his head. "It's driving people mad."

"Slowly, but surely," said Gabby.

Pedestrians avoided Stan - *watch out for the homeless kid acting weird and talking to himself* - a man growled at him, a woman clutched her handbag tight to her side muttering a prayer.

"There they are," said Gabby.

Across the road, alongside the entrance to the metro, stood four deathlings. A candle, two crumples and Clifford. Stan and Gabby crossed the road.

"This is Wes, Sally and Rahim. Clifford you know," said Gabby.

Stan nodded. The *floater* looked as nervous as ever. "Son of Death or not, jumping out a window was a stupid thing to do," said Clifford, water tumbling from his lips.

"I thought Blink was a traitor," said Stan.

"Well, he wasn't. We haven't seen him since he went looking for you," said Clifford.

The other three deathlings looked at Stan with something approaching awe: *this is the son of Death!*

"Still no sign of Blink then?" said Gabby.

Clifford licked his lips and rubbed his face. He looked at his watch. "No. Do you think they have him?"

"We can't wait to find out," said Gabby. "Joe?"

Stan felt himself go cold inside as Clifford glanced at him and then back to Gabby.

"Clifford, do you know something?" said Gabby.

Clifford shook his head. "Sorry."

Gabby's chin fell to her chest. She took a deep breath. "Let's go then. We have to assume we're all that's left." She turned away without meeting anyone's gaze.

The deathlings followed her into the metro's ticket office. Stan bought a pass and followed them as they slid past oblivious ticket inspectors. Gabby had said the rendezvous with Herne would be in a secret, secure place, but Stan couldn't think of anywhere more open than this.

"Where're we going?"

"Down," said the *candle* called Wes, smoke uncurling from his nostrils, as they stepped onto the escalator.

"It's okay, Stan, they know what they're doing," said Gabby.

The tunnel's wall was covered by adverts for the novel *The Hourglass World*. At the bottom they followed the crowd and then turned into a narrow side tunnel ending at a locked door. Clifford slipped a key from his pocket, led them through and locked it behind them.

On the other side of the door was a different world. Instead of bright lights, white tiles and film posters, they found themselves in a narrow, brick-lined corridor lit by infrequent, strip lights.

"Access tunnel," said one of the deathlings. Stan couldn't tell who.

They wound their way through patches of light and shadow. Nobody spoke. Tube trains rattled down nearby tunnels and gusts of air tugged at their hair and clothes. Gabby brought up the rear, behind Stan, and the others were spread out ahead. Stan watched Clifford pat his pocket every few seconds and he wondered if the deathling was carrying a weapon.

Wes raised his hand, signalling that they should stop. "Heard something," he said, peering back past Stan into the darkness.

Stan smelt the candle's smoky breath. He listened, his pulse beating in his ear. Distant trains rattled and clanked. They moved on, but Clifford kept peering nervously over his shoulder. He patted his pocket and smiled at Stan. He guessed it was supposed to be reassuring, but anxiety twisted the expression into a grimace.

They arrived at another door. Again, Clifford produced a key and let them through. This time they found themselves on a deserted platform.

"This is one of the old abandoned stations," said Stan, his words echoing around the space. He could just make out the dirty outline where the metro logo had been removed from the wall.

None of the deathlings replied. They were looking down the length of the platform, lit by two flickering strip lights, to a door opening at the far end.

"Stay behind us." Gabby moved to the front of their group.

A tall, hooded figure stepped out of the shadows onto the platform and walked towards them.

"It's Herne," whispered Gabby.

The strip lights buzzed on and off and the figure appeared to be moving in stop motion. His face remained hidden in shadow. A train passed nearby and the draught of its passing raised dust from the tracks. Water dripped from a broken pipe into a puddle. The resistance deathlings shuffled nervously.

"Something isn't right," whispered Sally.

"Too right," said Rahim. "Why doesn't he show his face?"

"Steady," said Gabby.

A train thundered by in the next tunnel - *clickety-clack, clickety-clack* - and suddenly Clifford grabbed his pocket. He wasn't quick enough. A rectangular box jumped free, hit the ground and bounced towards the wall. Spluttering water as he dropped to his knees, Clifford scrambled after it. As the box struck the wall its lid popped free and a pair of eyeballs rose into the air.

"Run!" shouted Blink. "It's a trap. Clifford's a traitor."

In the same moment the wind of the passing train ripped the hood from the approaching figure.

"Moses!" Rahim's eyes were wild.

Ahead of them, Sergeant Moses pulled the cloak over his head and dumped it onto the platform. He laughed and slid two heartseekers from his chest. "Not what you were expecting? Well, it gets worse."

The door behind them slammed shut and Stan spun around to face a dozen deathlings, all brutally disfigured murders, crowding onto the platform.

For a couple of seconds, everybody froze beneath the flickering lights. Stan acted instinctively, pulling the lighter from his pocket and hurling it at the strip light between him and Sergeant Moses. His aim was true. The light exploded, showering glass and sparks and plunging the centre of the platform into deeper shadow.

"The tracks." Stan leapt down from the platform.

He landed on his hands and knees, close to the live *third rail* and scrambled away from it. It hummed with electricity. If he touched it he'd fry like a burger. He turned around. Gabby was still on the platform, a terrible, defeated look twisting her face.

"Gabby, come on!"

Heartseekers flashed down the platform, winking in and out of sight beneath the flickering lights, and slammed into Wes and Rahim. As they fell to the platform, their souls rose from their bodies, quickly vanishing in a fairy flicker of light.

"No!" screamed Gabby.

Sergeant Moses and his armbands lurched forwards and Blink charged straight back at them. He brought the big deathling to a halt, but all he could do was buzz around his face distracting him.

"Come on, Ginger! I'll have you!" shouted Blink launching himself at Sergeant Moses' face again.

Roaring, Sergeant Moses swatted at the eyeballs like insects. Blink darted in and out of the big deathling's reach, causing him to flail and roar even louder.

"Gabby, get out of here. Follow Stan!" yelled Blink.

In that instant, Blink's concentration wavered. Sergeant Moses lanced out his arms and grasped his eyeballs. With a terrible grin he started to squeeze. Blink screamed and then fell silent. Sergeant Moses opened his fist and the eyeballs hit the platform with a splat. Blink's soul rose into the air.

The scream roused Gabby from her paralysis. She lunged for Clifford, but spraying water, the floater stumbled backwards towards Sergeant Moses.

"Come *on!*" yelled Stan.

She looked around. Sally was wrestling two armbands that had sneaked up on them from behind.

"Go, I'll hold them off as long as I can," she said.

Sergeant Moses and the other deathlings were closing in. It was over. All that was left was to retreat.

She scrambled down onto the tracks and followed Stan as he sprinted towards the tunnel. Darkness swallowed them and Stan widened his eyes willing them to adjust to the gloom. Behind them, gravel crunched as deathlings dropped to the tracks.

"I've let you down," said Gabby. "Let us all down."

"Later," said Stan.

"It's over."

"We have to keep going or Blink's death, the others, that's all for nothing."

"I know ... I know." Her voice held no conviction.

The tunnel widened to accommodate two sets of tracks. A meagre illumination was provided by little lights embedded in the wall. Air surged against them.

"Train," said Stan.

They pressed themselves against damp bricks as a train hurtled by. The carriages were sardine tight with commuters. A woman saw him, her head snapping to the side as she tried to keep him in her line of sight. The train passed, chased by swirling air and then they were back in the quiet dark.

They started to run again, stumbling over gravel and sleepers, always conscious of the buzzing third rail. Laughter bounced down the tunnel in pursuit.

"Where to now, Seer?" shouted Sergeant Moses. "The resistance is finished. It's all over."

He laughed again, and the sound echoed back and forth in the tunnels.

Where was he? How close was he? Stan couldn't tell. Down the tunnel he saw another train's headlights approaching. A draft of wind pressed against his face.

"Across there, quick" said Stan, pointing. The headlights had revealed an archway cut into the curve of the tunnel. Just inside was a door labeled: *Maintenance.*

Carefully, they picked their way over the live rail to the opposite wall. *Clickety-clack, clickety-clack.* The train rattled closer.

"Not this time, Seer."

The voice came from behind them. Stan turned to face Sergeant Moses, heartseeker in hand, on the opposite side of the tunnel. The air forced ahead of the approaching train tossed his mop of red hair.

Stan took another step towards the door and Sergeant Moses shook his head.

"You know, I've dreamed about dragging you before Death, your *loving* father, so he could see what a disappointing creature he'd whelped, but you've this irritating habit of slipping through

227

my fingers, so I'm thinking it's best we end this here and now. No more messing, eh? Say goodbye to your girlfriend. Say goodbye to everything."

Sergeant Moses hurled the heartseeker.

# 25

The train roared over the tracks between them and Stan opened his eyes, hands clutching his chest. No heartseeker. No pain. Gabby was behind him pushing open the maintenance door.

A metallic screeching mixed with the roar of the passing train. Stan could see sparks arcing into the air on the other side of the carriages. The heartseeker was embedded in the side of train, slicing down its length like a can-opener through a tin of beans. The carriages were packed with screaming commuters and in the fleeting gaps between carriages Stan glimpsed Sergeant Moses' face and the terrible expression on it; he was smiling.

"Stan! Come on!" Gabby had opened the door.

He jumped through after her and they locked it with a big bolt. The train passed and they heard boots crunching gravel. The door rattled as Sergeant Moses tried to follow them. He was still laughing.

"Run," said Stan.

They found an iron, spiral staircase and started the long climb to the surface. Panting, they took two or three steps at a time, each footfall echoing up the stairwell. Stan kept glancing down into the metal spiral below, expecting to see a flash of red, or hear the thud of heavy boots. When they reached the top he was drenched with sweat. They emerged into the ticket hall at the next station along the route.

"What do you think you're doing!" said a ticket inspector.

Stan ignored him and dashed out into the street. Blinding light slammed into his eyes and he threw up his hands.

"We have to hide," he said.

Gabby didn't speak, but she followed him.

Dodging hooting traffic, they crossed the road and crouched down behind a low wall fronting an office building. Stan lay on his back catching his breath.

Bloody tears streaked Gabby's face. "It's over. He's won."

"Not yet," said Stan, levering himself up.

"There's nobody left."

"There's us."

"You gonna fight them all on your own?"

"If I have to," said Stan, ducking down. "Moses."

Carefully, Stan peered over the wall. Sergeant Moses, his armbands and Clifford, were standing in front of the station surveying the crowds. They crossed the road and stood no more then twenty metres from his hiding place.

"Seer!" shouted Sergeant Moses. "I know you can hear me. Even a rat like you can't have scuttled that far. Know this, it's over. It's done. You've lost. Herne can't help you now. I have him. I always have, just that he didn't know it. All that's left is you and the girl and we'll get her soon."

"I'm going to rule life and death as I see fit now. I'm going to make the world truly fear death again. Make them bow down and worship me like in the good old days. They're going to raise temples to me and grovel at the feet of my statue praying and there isn't anything you can do about it."

Sergeant Moses moved down the street and stopped by an old couple standing in front of a shop window. The woman was looking at the lampshades inside. The man, uninterested in furnishings, was watching the passing traffic. Both must have been in their seventies.

"I'll take souls when I decide. Me! I'm Death now and I don't have to listen to the Universe. I'll save those who show me respect, the rest ..."

He leant forward and placed his hands around the old man's throat. He choked and crumpled to the pavement, his soul rising into the air and breaking apart.

"Bernard?" said his wife turning round to find her husband vanished. She looked down and screamed. Pedestrians rushed to her side.

Laughing, Sergeant Moses reeled around her and stalked over to a homeless man, head down, hand outstretched for coins. Crouching, he placed the tip of a finger against the man's forehead. His eyes rolled up into his head and his body slumped to the pavement, legs beating against the concrete, then twitching to a halt. His soul rose after the old man's.

Sergeant Moses stood up and spun on the spot. "Do you see this, Seer. I can kill as I please. Kill until I have sated myself and quietened mankind's pitiful wail. Give yourself up and I will spare them. Persist in this defiance and I will continue to kill. Ten this hour. Twenty after two hours. Forty after three hours. You see how it goes. I will make this city run with blood. It's your choice. I'm not playing hide and seek no more. Come to me today. Let's make an end to this."

Signalling to his men, Sergeant Moses strode away.

Stan stared down the road. He could see Sergeant Moses' red tunic in the distance as the deathlings wove their way through the crowded streets.

"Stan, no," said Gabby, moving to block his path. "I won't let you do this."

A cold certainty gripped Stan. He felt calm. For once, Sergeant Moses had been telling the truth.

"I don't have any other choice. You just said yourself, he's won. Unless I face him, and defeat him. I can't let this day go on any more and I will not have people die because of me."

"He'll crush you."

"Maybe," said Stan. "Maybe I'll kill him."

Gabby laughed bitterly. "You don't even know where he is."

"That's the easy bit. I just follow him. He wants me to," said Stan stepping to the side of Gabby.

She blocked his path again. "You'll have to get past me first."

"You can't stop me."

"I can."

"What're you going to do, take my soul?"

"Please don't," she said.

He tried to dart past her, but she scuttled sideways to block his path. Passers by saw a scruffy, dirty faced kid talking to himself and dancing around on the street and gave him a wide berth.

"You don't have to do this no more, Stan. Just run and hide. You didn't ask for it. You don't owe me anything."

She threw her body in his path again and her pendant jerked free of her dress, the half-coin gleaming in the sun. He remembered Joseph surprising him in the woods, and his instinctive reaction. He remembered the white light and the images that ripped though his mind:

*A busy street with tall, grand buildings. Men wearing long, black coats and top hats. Walking sticks clicking against the pavements. Women with bonnets and wide skirts. A dark street. Gas lamps. Puddles of light. Horse drawn carriages clattering over wet cobblestones splashing him. A man slashing at him with a walking stick. The sting of polished wood on his skin. Losing his footing and falling backwards, stumbling into the road. A girl's voice. Screaming. Fingers grasping his sleeve. His momentum carrying both of them into the road. Into the path of a carriage and its iron-shod wheels. Onto his back, the wheels crunching over cobblestones and ...*

"I do owe you. I owe you more than you can know," said Stan.

"What do you mean?"

He took a deep breath. "I'm so sorry."

"What for?"

"I ... " The words just wouldn't come out. "I ... I ... you saved my life."

Gabby smiled sadly, shoulders drooping, tears in her eyes. She didn't speak for a long time. Finally, she looked up at him again.

"Okay. Let's do this together."

# 26

Stan and Gabby soon caught up with Sergeant Moses. He was singing an old army marching song and killing as he went. They watched him bend low to a pram, laughing as the baby's little soul rose and scattered. He murdered a police woman by placing his hands on her head. He killed toddlers, parents and pensioners. Soon a panic ran though the city as news of the random deaths spread.

Finally, they came to a skyscraper at the busy heart of the city. Sergeant Moses and his cohorts entered the building.

"My god," said Stan, craning his head to look up above the building.

"What?" said Gabby.

He pointed. "Can't you see it?"

"See what?"

"Above the skyscraper."

Gabby shook her head.

It could only be his *vision,* whatever made him the Seer, that allowed him to see the amazing, pitch-black structure, that had fixed itself to the top of the skyscraper. Like a parasite, it held itself in place with six great arching struts that resembled insectile legs, before climbing twice as high as its host. Where the skyscraper was blandly rectangular, the parasite building was voluptuously curved like an immense cocoon.

They entered the skyscraper through a revolving door. Men and women in suits gave Stan quizzical looks and a security guard set off to intercept him. Muzak hummed in the background and a water feature, a slanting, unsupported wall covered by a steady sheet of water, splashed in the centre of the lobby.

"Are you ready?" said Stan.

Gabby nodded.

Trainers squeaking, Stan sprinted across the lobby and vaulted over a set of low security gates.

"Stop him!" shouted the security guard, sprinting in pursuit and fumbling to insert his pass into the gates.

He was too slow. Stan and Gabby dived into an elevator and hit the top floor button. Stan's ears popped as they climbed ... 1 ... 2 ... 3 ... The elevator slowed and the door pinged when they reached 32. They exited onto a derelict floor. Looping cables hung down through missing ceiling tiles like entrails. Random tables and chairs sat lonely and dusty. Blinds covered the windows, with only the odd slat bent out of shape to allow beams of light to arrow into the gloom.

"Nobody fancied Death as an upstairs neighbour," said Stan.

Gabby smiled, but it was an empty expression.

"Higher," he said.

They found a set of stairs that led to the roof. When they pushed open the door, Gabby stepped back inside with a cry.

"I see it now."

"I can go alone."

Gabby licked her lips. "Let you steal all the glory?"

They climbed a wide set of steps that led up into the belly of the building.

"No guards?" said Gabby.

"He's waiting for us."

Stan had expected something dark and gothic, like the castles in the old horror films he and Kalina watched on YouTube, but the black building's interior was as blandly corporate as the one below. The walls were painted neutral colours and decorated with abstract art. There was only one corridor from the lobby and all the doors leading off it were locked. At the end of the corridor an elevator swished open. They stepped inside. The only lit button was for the top floor.

"Are you ready?" said Stan.

"No."

"Ditto."

Stan pushed the button.

The doors closed and they rose smoothly. Stan calmed his breathing. He glanced at Gabby. She was chewing her lip and stroking her pendant. She looked at him. He met her gaze and nodded. A bell rang and the elevator came to a standstill.

"Whatever happens I ..." said Gabby, unable to finish the sentence.

"I know," said Stan.

The doors opened and light flooded into the space. Stan and Gabby stepped out of the elevator. They found themselves in a

237

huge room, with tall, floor-to-ceiling windows forming three of the walls and offering vistas across the city. The space was furnished as an opulent apartment. At the centre two semicircular sofas faced each other around a low table piled with heavy books. Statues, some startlingly modern, others crumbling and ancient, were placed on plinths around the room. A circular fireplace beneath a gleaming chrome chimney hood stood empty and cold. Deep, patterned rugs decorated the wooden floor.

Sitting on the sofa, wearing an expression mixing fear and joy, was his mum. Directly behind her stood Sergeant Moses.

"You surprise me, Seer. I thought you might be too much of a coward to come," said Sergeant Moses.

Stan ignored him. He only had eyes for his mum.

"Stan." Lucy's tears spilled onto her cheeks. His name came out as half sob, half word.

He was striding towards her in a second, oblivious of the others, arms aching to hug her.

"No." Sergeant Moses shook his head. He raised his hands, fingers slightly curled, scant centimetres from Lucy's shoulders. "One more step and I take her soul."

Stan stopped.

"Good boy. Now back up and stand by your girlfriend."

Stan did as he was told.

"I'm so sorry, Stan," said Lucy. "For everything."

Sergeant Moses bent down, close to her ear. "I told you to keep your cake-hole shut, didn't I?"

Lucy glared at him.

"Didn't I!" he shouted, spittle flying.

238

Lucy bent her head away from him and nodded, her mouth clenched with anger.

"She can see us all now. Me, you too Gabby girl. I did that. I can make ordinary humans see us if I want to. I have power," said Sergeant Moses.

"Leave her alone," shouted Stan.

"Or what?"

When Stan didn't reply Sergeant Moses laughed. "Like to see where that power comes from?"

Moses didn't wait for an answer. He pulled a plastic controller from his pocket, pointed it at a curtained section of the room and pressed a button. Slowly, the curtains pulled back to reveal a hospital bed. The bed held a tall, dark haired man with an olive complexion. A tube ran from his arm to a drip, suspended on a stand next to the bed. He lay as still as a statue.

Stan felt the room turn around him. Even from this distance he could clearly see the man's face. It was the face from the photograph in the lockup. The man who ran towards him. It was Death. It was his father.

"Here we all are," said Sergeant Moses. "One big happy family."

"I'm here to give myself up," said Stan. "That's what you wanted isn't it? Let my mum and Gabby go. Start time again. Nobody else needs to die because of me."

"No," said Gabby. "This isn't what we planned. We haven't come this far just to give in."

"It's the only way," said Stan, turning his attention back to Sergeant Moses. He moved closer to the big deathling. "Nobody need ever know that I even existed. Nobody need ever know that I ..." Stan looked at his mum and then back at Death. "That he's my father."

Lucy turned her head to face Death for the first time. "Marcus, wake up! For the sake of the love you once had for me, wake up and help him."

Death remained motionless in the bed.

"Believe me. He won't ever move again. There's enough magic and drugs in him to sedate a small country," said Moses.

"Mum, it's okay. I know what I'm doing."

"How terribly noble," said Sergeant Moses affecting a posh accent.

"Stan, it's no use. Moses ain't going to stick to no deal," said Gabby. "All he knows is killing. Just like he killed my Joe."

"Joe? You'd better ask your boyfriend about little old Joe," said Sergeant Moses. "I think you'll find that bit of slaughter can be chalked down to him. Ain't that so, Seer?"

Silence fell on the room. Stan sensed Gabby tensing.

"Your men killed him," she said.

"Did they? Did they really? I know exactly who killed Joe on account of the murderer's conscience getting the better of prudence and causing him to spill his guts to Clifford. Who is one of my men."

"Liar!"

"Ask your boyfriend."

"I'm not stupid enough to fall for your mind games."

"Ask 'im! Go on, ask 'im."

Stan felt the weight of Gabby's gaze; heard her feet shuffling as she turned to face him. The time had finally come. "Stan?" she said.

Not meeting her eyes, he reached into his pocket, pulled out the half-coin pendant and held it up. "It was an accident, I ..."

"An accident?"

"Yes."

"How ..." Gabby's voice caught in her throat. Bloody tears spilled from her eyes. "How could you?"

"He surprised me."

"Surprised you. He was a little boy."

"I know ... I know."

Fist clenched, Gabby took a step towards Stan.

"I'm so sorry," said Stan

Bloody tears streaked her face. "My little Joe. Poor little lost Joe."

"Now you see what the Seer's really like, eh Gabby? He's a monster, just like I always told you he was. A dirty killer. All he wants is deathling blood up to his elbows. He wants us all gone. It don't matter to him if it's me or Joe. For 'im, the only good deathling is a dead deathling."

"That isn't true," said Stan. "Gabby you know that isn't true."

"Shut up," shouted Gabby twisting to face him. Her eyes were pools of blood. She turned back to Sergeant Moses.

"That's it Gabby girl, you tell him." Sergeant Moses laughed. "You understand now don't you?"

Slowly, she nodded.

"Good girl." Sergeant Moses reached up and pulled a heartseeker from his chest. Blood oozed from the wound. He tossed the dagger to Gabby. She caught it and stared at the bloody blade.

"Now you know what happened to your poor little Joe. It's only right and proper that I give you the chance for revenge." Sergeant Moses smiled. "Kill him."

# 27

"Gabby, no," said Stan.

Sergeant Moses laughed as Stan backed away from her, glancing over his shoulder at Death.

"Please, I know you can hear me. Help me."

"He don't seem to be listening, Seer, maybe you need to talk *louder*." Sergeant Moses shouted the last word.

"Please! Father!"

"Father!" laughed Sergeant Moses, slapping his hands on the table. "See how desperate he's getting. Finally admitted what he is, but he don't understand one damn thing, Gabby girl. Can't even see what's before his porky-pies. Death ain't going to help you, boy. He ain't in charge any more is he. I am. I'm numero uno! Have been for thirteen years. Since you bawled your way into this world." Sergeant Moses pointed at Gabby. "Hold off for a second. I want him to hear this before he dies."

Gabby halted her pursuit of Stan, but kept her bloody gaze fixed on him.

"Death's lost his mind. He ain't nothing but a battery, I fuel myself with his energy. He lived for thousands of years and never found love until he met Louise Stefanie Mather. *Ahhh!*" He gave Lucy a false, sickly sweet look. "What a touching story, eh? Love in the twilight of existence. Only problem was, he went and fathered himself a child with her."

"Now, I thought he'd see the madness in what he'd done. Who knows what powers this creature will have, I told him. He didn't like that. He refused to listen. He was in love and in love with the idea of this child. An heir for his empire."

Sergeant Moses spat on the floor and thumped his chest. "I was supposed to be his heir! Me. Years I'd served him. Learned all the lessons. Endured his worthy sermons about how we was saving humans. All these years of service were going to disappear without reward. Well, that happened to me in life, it weren't happening again in death."

"So I took the situation in hand. I tracked down this *love of his life* and I told her that Death wanted nothing to do with her. The baby had to die."

He bent low, his face alongside Lucy's head.

"She surprised me, this one. Not many I can't scare into doing my will. Not this one. She ran and hid. Hid both of you well."

As Sergeant Moses spilled the hidden history of his life, Stan desperately tried to think of a way to wake his father. Maybe all it would take would be a touch, but he daren't move as long as Moses stood so close to his mum. One touch and she was dead.

"In some ways, her escape was more powerful than any magic I'd learned. It broke Death's heart. She was gone. He'd lost her. He started to fade and he was no match for me then. That's when yours truly seized his chance. *Carpe Diem!* All my life I've had my ..." Sergeant Moses mouth twisted as he searched for the right word. "... *betters*, ignore me. They used me as a tool, a soldier. Somebody to kill and intimidate, a crude thing, but didn't pay no heed to my words, to my mind, 'cause I was low born. *Be seen not 'eard Moses, that's the way, old chap.* Well, not this time! This was my time. As Death faded, I bent *him* to *my* will and made him learn me everything. How to rule deathlings. How to listen to the Universe. How to control time. I learnt it all."

He smiled again. "While he still had some strength, I made him tell me the truth about how it all began. Had to make sure there weren't no nasty surprises that'd trip me up. Believe me, that was the most interesting revelation of 'em all."

Sergeant Moses' tongue caressed his widening smile as he savoured their anticipation.

"Deathlings is a lie," he said raising his arms laughing. "There's no need for us. When humans die, their souls find their way to Forever whether they drift apart straight away or whether they's guided by us. *We aren't needed.* Never were. We didn't exist until he came along. We were dreamt up by him. He ain't just your father, Seer, he's a father to us all. The funniest part of all is that the only souls that *do* need guiding are deathling souls, but we can't do that. No deathling can hold another deathling's soul. May as well try to hold mist. Nobody knows why, just the way it is. That means he's trapped us all here. What a hero, eh?"

Sergeant Moses looked over towards the bed. "There might be a tiny bit of him left in there, but that's all. Hard to believe, but he was a Roman emperor. The mightiest of men in life and the mightiest in death, until you came along and ruined him."

Stan stepped forward. "All you can do is scuttle around in his shadow like a coward."

"Seer found his voice again? How disappointing, it gives me an 'eadache."

"The truth hurts, doesn't it?"

"Shut your mouth," said Sergeant Moses in a bored voice. "Gabby, time to finish this murderer."

Gabby raised the knife, crooked fingers caressing its handle. Bloody tears streaked her cheeks as she slowly stalked him.

"I bet you were a coward in life too," said Stan, backing away. He needed to find the hook to drag Moses into a rage. He needed him to follow. Needed him closer.

"See these daggers? In my *front*. I ain't never turned tail in any campaign," he said curling a lip beneath his bushy moustache.

"You're just a bully. I know all about bullies. They all have one thing in common, they're cowards."

"You calling me a coward, Seer."

"Who else'd get a girl to do his dirty work but a coward." Stan spat on the floor. "Coward."

Sergeant Moses yanked a heartseeker from his chest, charging past Gabby and straight at Stan. Stan stumbled backwards across the room, eyes widening momentarily as he met Gabby's bloody gaze.

"How do you like this for cowardice," said Sergeant Moses raising the heartseeker to strike.

Lucy was on her feet, screaming, running down the room. She was too late. Sergeant Moses was on him.

The heartseeker's sister blade flashed from Gabby's hand accompanied by a shriek of pure desperation. For a second, it seemed impossible for Sergeant Moses to avoid its trajectory, but in life he'd been a soldier and his soldier's instincts had been preserved by death. He spun, his arm a blur, and blade met blade sending sparks flying. Gabby's dagger spun through the air and embedded itself, juddering, in the floor.

"Twice a traitor, Gabby. No third time lucky."

Gabby spat blood at Sergeant Moses as he launched the heartseeker at her. It struck her in the chest. With a scream, staggering backwards, legs crumpling, she collapsed onto the floor.

# 28

Sergeant Moses called the heartseekers home and spun around to face Lucy. He marched towards her, knife in hand. "Back!"

"Leave my son alone!" she yelled. "Take me. It's all my fault."

"I said: back!" Sergeant Moses forced her back to the sofa.

"Stan, run. Please just run." Tears streaked her cheeks.

For a second, Stan was immobile, unsure of what to do, but Gabby's gurgling sob, drew him to her side. Her hands were clamped over the centre of her chest, blood seeping between her fingers

She tried to speak but couldn't. Bubbles of blood appeared on her lips as she mouthed *sorry, plan failed.*

"Don't say that," said Stan, growling with frustration. He wanted to hold her, comfort her, but he knew he couldn't.

*Over ... Run.*

He shook his head. "I'm going to beat him. For Joe."

He'd apologised a hundred times to her since he finally confessed what had happened to Joe in the woods. As they'd tracked Sergeant Moses through the city, a fear of failure had grabbed him; a fear of unfinished business and loose ends. If he was going to die, it wasn't right that Gabby didn't know what had happened to her brother.

The confession rose into his mouth like bile. He spat it out. Gabby had been inconsolable, her face awash with bloody tears, words replaced by choked sounds as she collapsed onto the pavement. She'd refused to meet his gaze. Refused to speak to him. He told her repeatedly how sorry he was. Finally, in a tiny, broken voice, Gabby started to sing a lullaby. Stan couldn't catch half the words, but it was something about cradles, swings and starlight.

"Used to sing him to sleep with that when he was a little 'un," she said, wiping away tears, dragging in a rattling breath.

"If I'd have known who he was, what was happening ..." Stan's sentence dribbled away to nothing. He knew words could never salve her wound. Her brother was gone. They fell into silence.

"Weren't your fault was it," she said, finally. "He was just a monster to you."

Stan started to protest then stopped. "That's what I thought," he said. "At the time."

She nodded. "I should have done more. Should have got to you earlier. It weren't your fault."

Somehow her forgiveness made him feel even more guilty, but he didn't have time for such self pity. She was on her feet again.

"We need to go and get the person what's really to blame," she had said. "We can use this against Moses. Let me see his back for a second and it's over."

Now even that simple plan had failed.

Stan stood and faced Sergeant Moses. Behind him, black thunderheads hung over the city like the belly of a great beast.

The deathling smoothed down his bushy moustache, opened his arms wide and smiled at Stan. "Me and you, eh, Seer?"

"Let her go," said Stan, pointing at Lucy.

"You sure?"

"Let her go. Now."

"If you insist," said Sergeant Moses, shrugging, starting to turn.

"No! Not that!" Stan sprinted forward. He was too slow. Sergeant Moses shot out an arm and grabbed Lucy around the throat. She screamed and twisted to face Death, but Sergeant Moses choked off any appeal for help before it left her lips.

Her eyes found Stan's and they were more eloquent than any words. They spoke of regret, pride, guilt and most of all, love. Then, life deserted them and they were no more than jelly and lenses. She slumped to the floor. Sergeant Moses stood above her gripping a blazing sphere of light and pulled back his arm.

"Catch," he said, as he hurled Lucy's soul down the room.

Stan launched himself sideways, arm stretched and fingers grasping, but his reach wasn't long enough. The light arrowed past his fingertips and vanished through the wall at the far end of the room. He landed on his hands and knees. He could see his mum lying dead on the floor.

"No!"

Sergeant Moses stalked towards him.

"You're dead," yelled Stan jumping to his feet.

Sergeant Moses laughed. "Have been for over an 'undred years, but that's the spirit!"

He drew two heartseekers from his chest. As he launched the first dagger, Stan reacted instinctively, concentration fuelled by his rage. The blade seemed to slow in the air. His mind raced, predicting the trajectory, plotting a reaction. His right hand flashed out connecting with the heartseeker. It spun wildly across the room and smashed through one of the massive windows. Shards of glass rained down on the streets below and wind howled into the room. Thunder boomed loud and near. They were almost high enough to be in the clouds. The heartseeker arced back, smashing through another window, and returned to Sergeant Moses. Distant screams rose from the streets far below as the lacerating debris reached the ground.

Stan cradled his hand. The blade had slashed his palm and blood ran freely from the wound, dripping from his fingers.

"Sharp ain't they?" said Sergeant Moses. This time, grunting with exertion, he hurled two daggers.

Stan stumbled backwards, towards the smashed window. The heartseekers were a blur. He could barely track them. He threw out both arms, yelling in pain as the daggers spun away from him again. He grasped his left hand. It felt wrong, incomplete. He looked down. His little finger was lying on the floor, cleanly severed. Blood poured from the remaining stump. Memories of the severed sausage-finger flashed into his mind. Kalina - he was never going to see Kalina again. His mum was dead. He was going to fail.

The room filled with the photoflash brilliance of lightening. Thunder followed, loud enough to shake free more glass from the shattered windows. Wind roared rain through glass fangs. Stan climbed to his feet. The second dagger had sliced into his shoulder and a fiery pain radiated from the wound.

"Father. I know you're in there. You called to me from the photo."

Death remained as still as stone. He was burnt out and empty. Stan was alone.

He yelled and sprinted straight at the deathling. He knew it was a suicide charge, one touch and his soul would be ripped from his body, but he ached to feel his fingers squeezing Moses throat, even if it was for the briefest moment.

With practised ease, Sergeant Moses dropped into a fighting stance and thrust a dagger at Stan's heart. Stan's momentum almost carried him onto the dagger's point, but at the last moment, twisting and shifting his weight, he threw himself to the side. The blade sliced through his T-shirt and across his chest. Instantly, blood soaked into the fabric. He caught his head on the side of the table and saw stars as he crashed onto the floor. Pain radiated through his body. Stars danced in his vision.

Sergeant Moses swept in for the kill. He raised a dagger. Held it above his head, two handed. Red hair swirling around his face in the wind. Down came the dagger, his red eyes reflecting a flash of lightening so bright Stan had to blink.

In that momentary blindness, a figure appeared behind Sergeant Moses. Through the lightening's retinal ghost image, Stan saw the figure as a silhouette. The silhouette threw its arms around the deathling, pinning his arm to his sides. The downward motion of his arms drove the heartseeker deep into the meat of his own thigh.

Sergeant Moses screamed, then snarled as he tried to wrestle free of the hold.

"Son, quickly," said the silhouette.

"No! You're mine!" shouted Sergeant Moses renewing his attempts to free himself. "You're nothing but a bag of bones."

"I was a human once," said the silhouette. "Love is the human's greatest magic. Stronger than any you possess."

As Stan's eyes cleared, he saw Death, arms wrapped around Sergeant Moses.

Death looked down at his son. His dark eyes had come to life, swimming with the wisdom and pain of two millennium's existence. His face twisted with exertion as he tried to hold onto his nemesis.

"I cannot restrain him for long," said Death, as Sergeant Moses thrashed his head back and forth trying to smash it into Death's face. "You have come to me, as I knew you would. Now the great lie has to end. You have to use your true powers."

Stan used the table to haul himself to his feet. His four fingered hand slipped on the wood. "What powers?"

"There is one piece of knowledge Moses never tortured from me. Your true gift."

"What do you mean?" Stan's head throbbed with pain. Death's words made no sense.

"Deathlings have the power to take a human's soul. *You* have the power to take a deathling's soul, and to guide it to Forever. You can do what no deathling can do. You aren't our doom. You are our saviour."

"No!" screamed Sergeant Moses redoubling his efforts to escape.

Stan looked down at his bloodstained, maimed hands.

"That's why you were sent to us. To save us from the nightmare I created."

"No! Don't you dare touch me," yelled Sergeant Moses, kicking out at Stan. "This is my time. My time, god damn you."

As the big deathling raged and writhed, Death brought him to his knees with a sweep of one leg and dropped down alongside him.

Stan stood before Sergeant Moses and raised his unharmed hand. The deathling leant as far away from his hand as Death's grip allowed.

"Take his soul," said Death. "Show it to Forever."

"How?"

"You will know. You already did it with Joe, purely by instinct"

"I guided Joe to Forever?"

Death nodded.

Gabby let out a yell mixing pain with elation. "Take him. End it," she said.

Stan looked into Sergeant Moses' eyes and his hand froze. All the arrogance and cruel bravado that had glittered in the deathling's bloody gaze had been snuffed out.

"Not got the balls for it," said Sergeant Moses.

"You're scared," said Stan.

"I ain't afraid of nothing, nothing I tell you! I was at the Khartoum with Gordon. I wasn't afraid when they came for us across the White Nile, screaming like devils, thousands of the buggers. Did I run? I did not. Sergeant Moses ain't afraid of nothing."

"Except for the unknown," said Death. "That's why you couldn't cross to Forever when you died, Robert?"

"Don't you dare use my given name. You ain't got the right." Sergeant Moses thrashed left and right trying to bite Death.

"Son, you have to do this. We have to undo his work. We must mend the broken day before it's too late."

Stan turned his gaze on the broken windows. Outside the storm still raged, lashing the city with its fury. He turned back to Sergeant Moses.

"This is my time! My time! It ain't fair."

Stan reached out and grabbed Sergeant Moses' throat.

A searing pain ripped down his arm. White light roared into his mind, consuming everything, then peeled back to ...

# 29

*Darkness. A dry, hot night.*

*You're standing on sandstone steps, holding a rifle fitted with a bayonet. Below you, half a dozen red-jacketed soldiers with rifles form a semi circle, protecting the base of the steps. Above you, flaming torches are held by more men. A dusty square lit by bonfires ahead. Gunfire all around. The screams of the wounded and dying. You can smell smoke, cordite, open latrines and rotting bodies.*

*They've broken through the wall, somebody screams and suddenly soldiers are fleeing past you, throwing down rifles, faces rigid with fear. The soldiers at the foot of the stairs, look up at you, hesitate, then flee with their comrades. Cowards, get back here! Your words have no effect.*

*An older soldier appears at the top of the steps. His uniform is ornate. Golden braids on the shoulders. Medals on his chest. A neat, waxed moustache curling up at the end. The expression on his face is an equal mixture of serenity and arrogance. He holds a sword. The blade reflects the dancing*

*flames. You feel a deep resentment of the man, at the same time as*
*a devotion bordering on love. You hate these feelings.*

*General Gordon, I told you they'd break through, you say.*
*Not enough gunboats. That was the time to retreat.*

*The General looks down at you, strokes his moustache,*
*doesn't speak. Anger flickers in his eyes at the word retreat, then*
*they snap up to take in the square. They have come for you. A wall*
*of screaming enemies. Robes flow as they charge forward. Snow*
*white turbans. Swords and spears.*

*You fight for as long as you have strength. There are too*
*many of them. Eventually they drag you from the steps. You see*
*the General fall. His head held high on a spear. Then an old, one-*
*eyed warrior squats over you and draws daggers from the sash*
*around his waist. The hilts are ornately carved and shine bright,*
*alive with fire. You've learnt something of the local language.*
*You're clever. Your superiors didn't care. You were born poor. The*
*rank of Sergeant should be good enough for the likes of you.*

*He fights like a devil. You need magic daggers -*
*heartseekers - to kill a devil, says the one-eyed warrior. Others*
*urge him on. You curse them. Then the blades fall, slide*
*effortlessly into your chest ... One ... Two ... Three ... So sharp you*
*don't feel them steal your life.*

*The square is fading. So are the screams. It isn't fair. The*
*pompous asses should have listened to you, they should have ....*

Suddenly Stan was back in the tower, Sergeant Moses' soul
a ball of light in his hands. Death was slumped against the wall,
panting with exhaustion.

"Send it on its way."

"Why should we save him?"

"We show mercy so we don't become a monster like him."

Stan nodded. The words were a relief. Now his rage had evaporated, his former bloodlust made him feel nauseous. He starred at the ball of light. Its brightness etched dark lines onto his retina. He opened his hands and the ball of light floated free. He willed it into the air. Beyond it, an intense light consumed the ceiling.

"Guide him," said Death.

With a thought, Stan moved the sphere towards the brightness. It fought him, trying to return to its body, to hold on to its existence, but it could not resist Stan's power. It floated upwards, picking up speed, as if conquering fear and slowly merged with the light. When they were as one, the light folded in on itself, like a puzzle with too many dimensions, and all that remained was the ceiling.

"It is done," said Death turning a weary head towards Lucy's body. A sigh chased tears from his body. "I always loved her. I'm so sorry I couldn't save her, then and now. Go to her. I must try to undo Moses' madness and reset the broken day while there is still time."

As Death's face screwed up in concentration, Stan clambered to his feet, cradling his maimed hand, and crossed to his mum. She'd fallen in an awkward tangle of limbs. He straightened out her arms and legs, brushed hair from her face. When he took her in his arms the tears came.

"Thank you," he said. "For keeping me safe and ...."

258

The lift doors opened and Clifford hurried into the room, bending his route and cowering as he passed Death.

"Stay away from me!" said Stan as the floater approached him.

"But ..." A spray of water shot from his mouth.

"Stay away!"

Clifford swallowed. Water dribbled down his chin as his mouth worked soundlessly. His hands were cupped together. He unlaced his fingers and white light lanced free. "I caught her soul."

"What?"

"Your mum's soul. I caught it when Sergeant Moses threw it away. I can put it back. Save her. I have to ... to make good what I've done." Water tumbled from his lips.

Stan looked across the room to Death. His eyes were still closed, face contorted with effort. "Is he telling the truth?"

Death nodded, opening his eyes. "It is possible. Be quick, before her soul breaks apart."

"If you try to trick me," said Stan lifting a threatening hand at Clifford.

Clifford knelt down alongside Lucy and pushed the ball of light towards her body. It wanted to rise and break apart, so he had to force it down, wrapping his fingers around it as if he was pushing a ball under water. When the light touched her flesh, it slowly flowed into her body. Clifford was careful to ensure his fingers didn't touch her. Suddenly, as if the body had decided to accept it, the rest of the light was sucked inside.

They waited. Seconds passed like minutes. Nothing happened. Stan looked up at Clifford.

"It works," said the deathling. "I've *seen* it work."

"Well, it isn't this time. Do you need to do something else?"

"No. That's it. Just return the soul, that's all you have to do, return it. The body does the rest."

She still wasn't breathing. "Mum, can you hear me?"

No answer.

"Mum ..."

Like a swimmer rescued from near drowning, she lurched back to life coughing and spluttering, drawing in ragged breaths. Her eyes were distant, unfocused. Stan threw his arms around her and confused she tried to wrestle from his grip.

"The light ..." she said.

"It's okay. It's over." He hugged her tight and slowly her thrashing stopped. Her eyes found focus on his face.

"Stan. You saved me."

Stan shook his head. "Clifford."

The floater was already backing away.

"Son, quickly." Death was calling him.

He stood and helped Lucy to her feet, glancing at Gabby. She'd dragged herself to the sofa and propped herself upright. "Go to him. I'll be okay. Moses didn't hit anything necessary. Tough as old boots me."

Stan hesitated. He knew she was lying.

"Help Gabby," he said to Clifford.

"Herne can help her," said Clifford, running back to the elevator. "Moses' gone. Nobody'll stop me freeing him now."

Stan knelt by Death. "What's happening to you?"

Death's body had undergone a rapid deterioration. He was losing muscle tone and clumps of hair rested on his shoulders. His skin was turning grey and his eyes filling with blood.

"Moses did something to me ... linked us ... fed off my power ... I'm fading."

"No. You can't. "

"Listen to me, son ... important. Do exactly what ... I say. Not strong enough anymore." Death's voice was a whisper. "I can't heal time ... not alone and ..."

Stan sensed Lucy standing behind him. Death looked up at her. It took a great effort to move his head. He opened his mouth but no words came out. A single blood-tear ran down his cheek.

"My love," he said.

"Marcus."

"Forgive me. I should have stopped him."

Lucy nodded, struggling to form her own words. Finally, she said: "It wasn't your fault."

"I always loved you," he said

"I know."

He smiled and a coughing fit took hold. When he pulled his hands away from his mouth they were smeared with blood and a tooth sat on his palm.

Death looked up at Stan. He was panting. His cheeks were cracking and spilling clear fluid.

"Running out of time. Place your hands on me ... now."

"Why?"

"Need your strength ... your power to restart time."

"What'll happen to you?"

Death shook his head. "Doesn't matter."

"I'll take your soul, won't I?"

"Do as I say."

"I've only just found you."

Death took a deep breath, gathering his remaining energy. "I called to you and you came. Now you have to undo everything I have done. Start with the broken day ... we fix that together. When I'm gone ... you ... stop the suffering."

"But."

"Ask Herne, he'll guide you. You can ... heal everything."

"I won't take your soul," said Stan, standing and stepping away.

Death coughed again. "It's me or the world."

"I won't chose," he said, but his voice held no conviction.

"You will. That's why I know you are my son. That's why I love you." Death held out his arms. "Promise me you'll help the others when I'm gone."

Stan knelt by Death.

"Promise me."

"I promise."

"At least I will be able to hold you this one time."

Tears filling his eyes, Stan lurched forward and embraced his father, gripping him tight. He opened his mouth to reply, but it was too late. As they touched, pain and searing white light detonated throughout his body. His words exploded into a scream ....

*Somebody is screaming. You turn on the spot. Where is the scream coming from? You're standing in a high ceilinged room edged by marble pillars. An ornate mosaic depicting a hunting scene beneath your feet. It's night. The room is lit by lanterns. The air smells oily, and smokey. A desk before you. Rolled scrolls. You're wearing a toga. It feels heavy on your shoulder. You're sweating. Your stomach gurgles and a pain knifes your guts. You bend over to catch your breath and slowly straighten up.*

*The screaming is closer. Somebody saying your name repeatedly: Marcus ... Marcus ... Marcus! You recognise the voice.*

*Stomach cramps double you over. You glance at a plate on the table. It's empty save for chicken bones and olive stones. A spasm shakes your body and you begin to tremble as if you have a fever. You look at the plate again. The chicken hadn't tasted right, but you'd been too hungry, too pushed for time as you read petitions from the Senate, to send for something else.*

*Marcus! Your sister Olivia runs into the room, all wild hair and wilder eyes. She's the screamer. She looks at the plate then back at you. She's gasping for breath. Oh, my dear Marcus. Jupiter save us. It was poisoned.*

*Her words are like a catalyst to the toxin racing through your body. Pain twists the knife in your stomach again and you collapse to the floor groaning. You're panting, dripping with sweat. Olivia's cool hand strokes your brow. I'll call the priests, she says.*

263

*No time you say. It is done. She weeps as she embraces you.*

*You no longer feel your limbs. Your vision has grown dim.*
*You're calm. You had many political enemies and they wanted you*
*dead. You knew it might come to this. You prepared. Prepared for*
*an early death with magic.*

*Pain spears through your kidneys and your back arches.*
*Spittle foams on your lips. You hear your sister praying.*

*Your eyes close.*

*You leave the world.*

*You are rising, a ball of light floating heavenwards. Above*
*you an immensity of light calls to you. Summons you. Waits to*
*envelop you. Let go, it says. Release yourself.*

*You resist. Across the globe you have fought battles and you*
*have never lost. You will not lose this battle. You have gathered*
*every magician, shaman and mystic from across the world-*
*spanning breadth of the Roman Empire and forced them to teach*
*you the secrets of life beyond death. Runes had been tattooed on*
*the inside of your skin. Dragon tears have cleansed your eyes. You*
*have drunk the blood of ghosts and bathed in black rain.*

*When the light withdraws, you are left standing over your*
*own, dead body. Your sister hugs your corpse and weeps. You say*
*her name but she cannot hear your words. Armour rattling,*
*legionnaires run into the room, straight past you and look down at*
*your dead body. Your sister screams at them to leave ... to stay ...*
*to call the priests ...*

*You laugh and dance around the room. You have won. You*
*have cheated death. Now, you have become Death. Now it is time*
*to build your new empire.*

Stan started to emerge from the trance, but he couldn't open his eyes. Machines ... he could hear machines starting up; a deep, throbbing, churning sound, rising in intensity. He thought back to the night when the day had broken, the terrible headache that had almost split his skull open as time ground to a standstill. This time the feeling was the opposite. He felt weightless and giddy as if oxygen were being pumped into his body. Louder and louder sounded the engines, gaining a steady rhythm and then ...

... he opened his eyes. A ball of light nestled in his cupped hands. His mum was standing by him.

"You did it," said Gabby, still on the floor, leaning against the table.

Stan looked out through a broken window. The storm had finally stopped and the city was calm.

"Let him go, Stan. He's ready now," said Lucy.

Stan staggered to his feet. Wind buffeted him as he leant out of a broken window and released Marcus' soul. It floated skyward, climbing towards the retreating clouds. He urged on the soul and it sped through the air as the clouds broke apart above it. Sunlight arrowed down on the city, mixing with an even more intense light spreading wide to welcome Marcus. Stan squinted and shielded his eyes. He couldn't see his father's soul. He'd passed to Forever and all that remained was sunlight.

Stan embraced his mum, squeezing her until she groaned. "Thank you," he said.

"You saved me, silly boy," she said, laughing and crying.

"All those years."

"I'm your mum."

The lift door opened and Clifford led a group of deathlings into the room. Two dashed to Gabby's side. Clifford led a tall twig with swirling tattoos on his cheek to Stan.

"This is Herne," he said.

"Finally we meet," said the deathling with a small bow.

Stan remembered his father's words: *stop the suffering*.

"I need your help," said Stan.

"I know," said Herne.

# 30

Stan shared the brow of the hill with his mum, Gabby and Herne. It seemed right that the journey should end where it had begun, all those long days ago, when he first saw the deathling horde assembled. Surrounding the hill like a sea they had gathered again; every deathling created by Death in this one place. Their voices ebbed and flowed like a tide beneath the cloudless night sky.

His father had said: *stop the suffering*, and Stan knew what he had to do. The Seer's powers weren't a curse, they were a *gift*. Now was the time to use that gift. Alone with Herne in the aftermath of the battle with Sergeant Moses, Stan had explained his plan.

"This is what I have desired through the long years of my captivity," said Herne. "But I cannot ask this of you. It must be freely given. What you would undertake is very dangerous. It could cost you your soul."

"I promised my father." Herne started to protest, but Stan interrupted him. "I promised."

The twig sighed deeply. "Then I thank you for your courage, Stan Wisdom."

Herne summoned the deathlings to the park. He spoke to them, without pause, for an hour. The power of his voice and the force of his story telling belied his feeble appearance.

He told the deathlings the truth of their existence. How Death had come into being by magic; how he'd lied about the need to save souls, desiring a new empire to rule, and subjects to populate that empire. A population to obey his orders and worship him. How they'd all endured an eternally painful existence without cause. Human souls did not need to be guided to Forever. Deathling labours, and suffering, had been without any point.

Only deathling souls needed a guide, but deathlings couldn't do this themselves. Only the Seer could guide them.

At this, a great agitation spread through the crowd. Deathlings shouted denials and disbelief. Arguments raged back and forth. Fights broke out and groups of deathlings split off, making for the exit, only to turn back at the gates. He calmed them with his words.

There was no need to be scared. Forever welcomed everybody, said Herne. They'd all been scared when they died but the time for fear had passed. Now was the time to end their suffering and to accept what came next, the great mystery of Forever.

We must put this to a vote, he told them.

When Herne stopped speaking, a great hubbub rose from the deathlings as they rushed to form groups to debate the proposal.

"I'm scared," said Gabby.

Herne had treated Gabby's wound, but she hadn't recovered from its effects. Her body seemed even more crumpled than before and her voice had lost its spark.

"So will you vote 'no'?" said Stan.

She shook her head. "I'm too tired to carry on. Tired of the pain. Anyway, no point is there. Humans don't need us. It's like being a doctor when people don't get sick. Pretty stupid."

"You thought you were saving people."

"*Thought*. We were wrong."

"Doesn't matter. You did a good thing. You helped people."

"I suppose we did."

They fell silent, listening to the deathlings' debate, then Gabby spoke again. "What do you think it'll be like? You know, Forever?"

"Big?" said Stan

The ghost of a smile curled her lips. "Probably the best way to find out would be just to go and take a look."

"Sounds like a plan."

"Do you fink I'll find Joe?"

"I'm sure you will."

"Hope so."

Soon afterwards, Herne called the vote. A forest of arms were raised. The deathlings had voted *yes* to leaving earth. The empire of deathlings would end tonight.

"Are you ready, Stan Wisdom?" said Herne.

"I'm ready."

"Then let us begin."

Herne turned back to the deathlings and his voice rang out clear across the park. "Say your farewells and join hands."

Stan turned to Lucy and hugged her. She tried to release him, but he clung on to her. When he finally let go, she grabbed his shoulders and looked into his eyes. "This is safe, isn't it? You know how to control what's going to happen?"

"Of course," he said. He drank up the image of her face, not expecting to see it again and turned back to the sea of deathlings. He swallowed and squeezed his shaking hands into fists.

The deathlings had done as Herne instructed, forming a single chain, hand to hand, that snaked around the park, joining them all. The final links of the chain ran up the hill to Herne and ended with Gabby.

"I always wanted to give you a hug," she said, as he stepped forward.

"Tell Joe I'm sorry."

"Go on, hurry up, I can't take any more waiting."

"You sure?"

"Sure as eggs is eggs," she said, smiling.

Taking a deep breath, Stan leant forward and hugged Gabby. For one moment he felt her skinny, bony frame, felt her hugging him back with one arm and then white light and pain consumed him totally and ...

*... you are somewhere else: a busy street with tall, grand buildings. Your brother, Joe, strides along besides you. It's dark. Gas lamps hiss and cast puddles of buttery light. Horse drawn carriages clatter over wet cobblestones splashing you. The toffs in*

*their fine clothes look at you with hard faces and you quickly move out the way.*

*You're whispering to each other, giggling at a joke, and you don't see the tall man.*

*"Out of the way wretch!" he snarls slashing at Joe with his walking stick.*

*Joe cries out as he loses his footing and stumbles into the road. You scream and reach out for him, grabbing a sleeve, trying to haul him back, but his momentum drags you forward. You slip on the rain slick pavement. You're falling forward with him, you can't stop yourself, off the pavement and into the road. Into the path of a carriage and its iron-shod wheels. Onto your back, the wheels crunching over cobblestones and ...*

After that, images flowed together one after another ...

*Your frail body is lying on a bed of ferns on the brow of a hill. The country you love spread out around you. Below are the forests. Broad. Endless. A circle of men and women wearing green cloaks and crowns of leaf, twig and fungus stand around singing a lament in deep voices. You're climbing a mountain, baboons watching you with malicious eyes from their rock perches. Shale slides from beneath a foot and you lurch backwards. Your hand shoots out but all it finds is sappy plants. The world spins by in a blur as you fall. You're walking home from school down a dusty path winding across the savannah, laughing and joking with friends. You see a giraffe in the distance. Acacia trees dot the landscape. You slump beneath one for a rest. You don't see the snake until it strikes. Its venom races through your body and your eyes cloud over. You're sitting on your horse, gripping the reins so tight your hands are white as bone. Before you the countryside, once postcard-pretty, is mud, water filled craters, zigzagging trenches and miles of barbed wire. A whistle blows and you move forward at a canter, picking up pace, trying to charge through the mud. Machine guns rattle into life spitting bullets and you're punched from the saddle by a dozen hits. You land in bloody mud. Your horse lies next to you screaming. You close your eyes and think of your wife.*

The images come faster and faster, ripping through Stan's mind like speeded up film. So many images, so many lives. The heat of their passing shaking loose the very atoms of his being.

*You're wrestling with the controls of a small plane as it spirals from the sky above a large crowd at an air-acrobatics show. You're standing in the crowd at an air-acrobatics show staring up at a small plane spiralling down towards you. You're crushed against a fence in a football stadium. You're slamming a foot against your car's break pedal as you skid towards the back of a lorry. You're shouting at somebody then clutching your chest, a pain in your heart. You're lying in a hospital bed listening to the beep of monitors, nurses' chatter, birds singing and then you're gone. You're falling from the top of a pyramid. You're choking on a gobstopper. An avalanche smashes you beneath its icy fist. You're struck by lightning. A horse kicks you in the head. You fall off a motorbike. You're in a western gunfight, a car crash,*

*trampled beneath a Maharajah's elephant, in a submarine*
*trapped at the bottom of the sea slowly filling with icy water, a*
*tree falls on you a rat bite stings a priest dabs oil on your*
*forehead a painted-face man lunges at you with a knife you're*
*chokingdrowningsuffocatingbleedingfadinglaughingcryingdying...*
*..............*

*Now the images are a blur, pure energy racing through your*
*mind. You can't control the flow, can't grasp them. They're a beam*
*of energy smashing into you. You're vibrating, screaming,*
*stretching, breaking, atoms drifting apart.*

*Suddenly there's a bright light ahead. The light is warm. It*
*calms you, even as you drift further apart. It calls to you.*

*Give in.*

*Don't struggle.*

*Come to us.*

*Surrender ... surrender to the light.*

*You drift forwards, towards the light. Your atoms are*
*scattering. You know you're going to become one with the light. It*
*will be good to rest. To stop being ...*

*To end.*


"No," shouted Lucy, cradling Stan's body.

He'd stopped breathing. She lay him on the ground and blew into his mouth, hot tears on her face - one, two, three, four. When she stopped his chest remained motionless. She repeated the mouth-to-mouth. His body remained limp, lifeless.

"No," she said. "Stan come back. Please come back."

Leaning over him, she laced her fingers together, palms outwards, and pressed hard against his chest - one, two, three, four. She alternated the cardiac massage with mouth-to-mouth. She lost track of time. Her arms and lungs were burning with exertion. Eventually, she collapsed onto the ground alongside him and sobbed. He was dead. After everything he had been through, her son was dead. She lay back and covered her eyes with her hands.

"I heard you calling." The voice was so weak, Lucy thought she might be imagining it. She rolled onto her side. "Stan!"

"Look," he said, pointing. The night sky was full of floating souls. Thousands of globes of light slowly rising into the darkness like a new galaxy; a Milky Way of the dead. The heavens opened, white with pure energy. With the last of his strength, Stan urged the souls on.

"Don't be scared," he said. "It's over."

One by one they passed into the light and the brightness started to unravel into glowing filaments. For a few seconds, the sky looked like it was carpeted with gold, then the filaments faded to darkness and the night sky was returned to the possession of the moon and stars. The ghost image of the lights haunted his eyes for a few seconds more and then they were gone.

"Goodbye Gabby," he said.

# Epilogue: Tomorrow

Somebody was ringing the doorbell. Stan woke, opened one eye and grabbed his alarm clock: 09:20 WED 13th APR. Heart racing, he sat up and grabbed the clock. He closed his eyes. Opened them again. The clock still said: 09:20 WED 13th APR.

He leapt from bed and dressed, falling over as he struggled to pull on his shorts with his bandaged hands. His mum was sitting at the kitchen table, scribbling in a note pad. She popped a piece of gum into her mouth and grimaced as she started to chew. *Stop Smoking Now!* read the gum packet.

"A good time to stop," she said.

"A new book?"

She nodded. "This time I don't even have to make up a story."

The doorbell rang again.

"Go on, answer it. Invite Kalina in."

Stan raced downstairs. He pulled Mrs Cumberbatch's newspaper from the letter box. The headline read: GOVT IN NEW SECURITY BLUNDER.

He opened the front door. Kalina was wearing an oversized Hellraiser T-Shirt that reached her knees, red leggings and yellow converse boots. Her purple hair had been gelled up into two, asymmetrical spikes. She was holding a copy of a bright red book - *The Hourglass World*.

"Yes!" said Stan taking in her changed outfit.

Kalina raised an eyebrow. "Everything okay? You're not usually so interested in my sartorial style, Stan Wisdom."

"Everything is very ..." Stan sought the right word. " ... tomorrow."

"Very *tomorrow*? You laugh at *my* use of English." She saw the bandaged hand he'd been hiding behind his back. "Oh my god, what happened?"

"I had an accident with a knife."

"Are you okay?"

Stan looked out into the street. Beyond Kalina, Mr Williams was leaving the house, whistling and swinging his arms. There were no bin men, no creeping cat, and after yesterday's storm all the blossom lay in drifts at the foot of the trees.

"I'm fine," he said.

"I worked on a great new scene last night," said Kalina. "All we'll need to make it work is a shop store dummy's arm and some fish guts."

Stan screwed up his face

"What's the problem, Spielberg? Gone squeamish?"

"Can we take a break from horror? Just for a while."

"Really?"

"Let's make a comedy. Come up, we can start writing some scenes now."

"Your mum won't mind?"

"Nope. There's been a few changes since yesterday."

They stepped inside.

"Do we really have to make a *comedy*?" said Kalina.

"Nah, just kidding," said Stan. "Let's finish Zoological Zombie Zone, I can feel Hollywood calling."

**THE END**

**Zoological Zombie Zone**

**An (unfinished) screenplay by**

**Stan Wisdom & Kalina Kowalski**

**1. Interior Living Room Evening**

A teenage BABYSITTER has a mobile phone glued to her ear and she doesn't appear to be taking any notice of a BOY and his DOG who are wrestling on the floor.

**BABYSITTER**

(talking into her mobile)

Uh uh, uh uh. No way! Get out of here. He did not say that?!

The **DOG** starts to bark.

**BABYSITTER**

(covering the phone and pointing at the kitchen)

Mutt. Garden. Now.

**BOY**

But ...

**BABYSITTER**

Five minutes. Or I'm going to make you watch Dancing On

Ice.

A whooshing noise and cut to ....

## 2. Exterior Garden Evening

The garden is a mess. Somebody's started digging a pond
but the job's half done. When the BOY opens the back door,
the DOG sprints for the hole.

**BOY**

No!

Flying mud hits the BOY in the face. He rushes after the
DOG. The DOG is digging around a stone at the bottom of
the hole. He pushes the stone aside and emerges with a
dirty bone.

**BOY**

That's minging, give it here!


The BOY tries to pull the bone from the **DOGS** jaws. The **DOG** growls and clings on to his prize. Finally the bone comes free and the **BOY** flies backwards landing on his bum in the hole.


**BOY**

Ouch! Idiot hound. My bone now.


The BOY pretends to eat the bone and the dog trots off sulking.


**BOY**

Bad loser.


The **BOY** pulls the stone from beneath his bum. It's a smooth stone the size of a side plate and has runes carved on it.

BOY

I bet Dad got this from the garden centre.


**3. interior kitchen evening**.

The BOY puts the bone in the bin, walks into the living room
and puts the stone on the dining table. The **BABYSITTER** is
still talking on the phone.


BABYSITTER

He did what? With who? Her? Really? Really, really?


The **BOY** rolls his eyes.


BOY

Is your mouth actually connected to your brain?

**BABYSITTER**

(covering the mouth phone's speaker)

What did you say?


**BOY**

(miming using a Play station controller)

I'm going upstairs to play a game.


**4. interior kitchen evening**

The **DOG** is sniffing the bin, whining. He starts to paw at it.


**5. Interior bedroom evening**

The **BOY** is playing a zombie shoot-em up. There is a clattering noise from downstairs. He pauses the game.


**BABYSITTER**

(voice from downstairs)

Come and sort your dog out. I'm on the phone.

**BOY**

(sotto voce)

Oh dear, I can't hear you.


He turns the game back on, squeezing the controller.
Gunfire rattles on the screen.


**BOY**

Die babysitter, die!


### 5. Interior kitchen evening

The **DOG** has tipped over the kitchen bin and fished out the
bone. He's licking out the marrow.


### 6. Interior bedroom evening

The **BOY** turns off the Playstation and lies on his bed. He
closes his eyes.

## 7. Interior kitchen evening

The **DOG** suddenly starts to cough and whine. It rolls over onto its side. It looks dead.

## 8. Interior bedroom evening

The **BOY** is asleep and dreaming. His eyes move rapidly beneath his eyelids.

## 9. Exterior A moor night

A **VIKING BOY** and a **WITCH** stand on a moor before a hole.

#### WITCH
Put the foul creature in the hole.

The **VIKING BOY** dumps a dog sized, cloth-wrapped bundle into the hole. The **WITCH** holds up the flat, rune-carved stone.

**WITCH**

Odin, give this rock your power! Keep this undead creature
quiet! Let its plague trouble us no more!

She places the stone over the bundle.

**WITCH**
(to **VIKING BOY**)
Bury it.

The **VIKING BOY** starts to push soil into the hole.

### 10. Interior Kitchen evening

The DOG's eyes open. It's eyes are blood red. It clambers
to its feet, slobber slipping from its mouth, hackles rising. It's
back from the dead. It's a ZOMBIE DOG.

### 11. Interior Living room Evening

The BABYSITTER is still on the phone.

**BABYSITTER**

Well, if it was me, and I know it's not, but I'm just saying if it was, like, I'd ... I don't know what I'd do.

She doesn't see the **ZOMBIE DOG** slouching into the room because she's peering between the curtains. Drool slides from the **ZOMBIE DOG'S** mouth and it growls, eyes flaring red. The BABYSITTER spins around.

**BABYSITTER**

Laters.

She cuts the connection on her call.

**BABYSITTER**

Nice doggy.

The **ZOMBIE DOG** charges at her.

## 12. Interior Bedroom Evening

A scream from downstairs wakes the BOY. He sits up blinking. There is a thump from downstairs.

## 13. Interior Landing Evening

The BOY creeps out onto his landing from his bedroom. From below comes the sound of feeding.

**BOY**
Hello?

The sound of feeding stops. Claws on laminate. The **ZOMBIE DOG** appears at the foot of the stairs, eyes glowing red. Their eyes meet.

**BOY**
The bone.

He turns and runs for his bedroom. We hear the snarling ZOMBIE DOG hurtling up the stairs.

### 14. interior Bedroom Evening

The BOY slams shut his bedroom door and wedges it closed with a chair. The weight of the **ZOMBIE DOG** slams into it setting the door rattling. The chair slides against the floor. The **BOY** grabs his mobile and dials.

**BOY**

(Shouting into the phone)

You gotta get round here. Now ... Listen it's...

The bedroom door bursts open. The ZOMBIE DOG sprints straight at the BOY.

### 15. Interior Another bedroom Evening

The **GIRL** has her mobile pressed to her ear. We can hear the tinny sound of a scream from its speaker.

**GIRL**

What's happening? Are you there? What's happening? Tell

me .....

We hear the buzzing of a disconnected line. Her phone beeps. She opens a picture message. It's a close up of red eyes. She jams her phone into her pocket (we hear the sound of a pistol being cocked). With a whooshing sound we cut to ...

**16. Interior Kitchen Evening**

The Boy has now become ZOMBIE BOY. His eyes are red. His skin is moldy looking and hanging off in strips. He rummages through the fridge. He finds a raw steak. The **ZOMBIE DOG** growls at him.

**ZOMBIE BOY**

Find own food! Out!

The **ZOMBIE BOY** opens the back door and the **ZOMBIE DOG** disappears into the night.

**ZOMBIE BOY**

(moaning)

Need more meat! Must feed.

He spies a long kitchen knife. He grabs it and spreads a hand out on the work surface. He cuts off a finger. He drops it into his mouth and chews, making sounds of delight. The phone rings and the **GIRL** leaves a message. She is out of breath; sounds like she's running.

**GIRL**

(voice on answerphone)

I'm nearly there hang on! I'm coming.

The **ZOMBIE BOY** SMILES.

## 17. Exterior Front Door Evening

The GIRL stands by the door. It is already open a crack.

She pushes it with one finger and it creaks open.

## 18. Interior Hallway Evening

Cautiously, the **GIRL** enters the house. A red eye watches her through a crack in the door.

## 19. Interior Living Room Evening

The girl creeps into the room. She doesn't see the **ZOMBIE BOY** hiding behind the door. He shambles towards her moaning and drooling, reaching out for her flesh.

### ZOMBIE BOY

Must eat flesh!

The **GIRL** scrambles away from him, jumping onto a sofa and then over the back.

**GIRL**

What're you doing? It's me. What happened to you?
Please ....


The **ZOMBIE BOY** continues his relentless pursuit. The
**GIRL** trips and the **ZOMBIE BOY** nearly grabs her. She
screams. She's backed up against the table, nowhere else
to go. She reaches behind wildly looking for something to
defend herself with. She finds the rune stone and lifts it to
strike the **ZOMBIE BOY.**

**ZOMBIE BOY**

(flinching away from the stone and hissing at the GIRL)
Aaaggghhhhhh!


The **GIRL** looks at the rune stone and steps forward
brandishing it. The **ZOMBIE BOY** backs away, moaning, an
arm across his face.


**GIRL**

Look at me.

The **ZOMBIE BOY** peers beneath his arm.

**GIRL**

Don't you know who I am? Don't you recognise me?

Slowly **ZOMBIE BOY** lowers his arm. He smiles. There are chunks of meat stuck between his teeth.

**GIRL**

(lowering the stone)

You do remember me.

It's a ruse. **ZOMBIE BOY** lurches towards her. With a scream she brandishes the rune stone again and backs-up **ZOMBIE BOY** into the corner of the room. She puts the rune stone in front of him and he presses his back against the wall trying to get away from it.

**ZOMBIE BOY**

(snarls out the words)

I eat you!

**GIRL**

No you won't because I'm going to help you.


The GIRL sits at the table opens a laptop. She starts to browse the web.


**ZOMBIE BOY** tries to squeeze past the rune stone but its magic holds him in place. The image on the witch on the moors flashes into his mind. The girl glances over her shoulder and then returns to surfing the web.


**ZOMBIE BOY** raises his leg and pulls off a trainer. He carefully lowers it to the ground, then with his toe, uses it to push the rune stone aside. Quietly he slips past the rune stone, grinning. His eyes fix on the GIRL'S exposed neck. He licks his lips and creeps closer, arms raised, teeth bared and ....


*...NOW ITS YOUR TURN TO COMPLETE THE SCREENPLAY! WHAT HAPPENS NEXT? YOU DECIDE. FINISH THE SCRIPT, SHOOT THE FILM ... OVER YOU TO SCORSESE AND SPIELBERG.*

# ACKNOWLEDGEMENTS

It's not easy being a writer of imaginative fiction, but it's probably even more difficult being married to one. While you're trying to make sure the bills are paid on time, and the house doesn't fall down around your ears, the writer in your life is likely to be staring into space imagining the exact topography of some imaginary realm or papering the house with Post-its scribbled with gnomic or alarming messages (... *book about vampires burnt by darkness ... man has fish for teeth ... hammers attack humans ... are balloons evil ...*) so foremost, thank you to my beautiful and tirelessly supportive wife, Tracy.

My mum and dad taught me to love books. Mum didn't live to see this published (I know she would have been proud) and I'm sure she'll be able to read it in Forever. Dad is the rock on which my personality is based - you need a firm, moral, down-to-earth base when your ideas can be wild. Thanks to my brother Neil, a talented artist, who designed my musingMonster Books logo.

Friends have politely listened to me banging on about writing for years and their support has been invaluable; so step forward Martin Whittingham, Paul Langham, Steve Doyle, Pete Bradbury and Andy Thums. A special mention for Mick Reader who always finds time to proof a manuscript even when his twins are trying to fill his nostrils with Play-Doh.

Thanks to the ever supportive Stan Griffin (a collaborator, drinking buddy and friend since our days editing rival football fanzines), and all the marvellous team he put together under the *Loop Productions* banner to make the ATDT's stunning promotional film.

My superstar niece Zehra Hewitt-Mustafa is one of my biggest supporters and collaborators - we've already written a dozen picture books together, but she's told me I need to work on my drawing.

My panel of young readers have been essential in writing (and rewriting this book). Nobody gives honest feedback quite like a kid. So thanks to Ciaran Bradbury-Hickey, Joe and Heidi Whittingham, Oliver and Bethany Thompson. A special mention to Stan Abbott-Stacey (future Team GB cycling star) who spent half an hour enthusiastically recounting this book's plot (he didn't know I'd written it) and letting me know he thought it'd make a good film.

A book without a cover is like a sandwich without bread ... so many thanks to Ellen Woodward for her beautiful external and internal art work.

Thanks to Julia Churchill for providing essential structural criticism and stopping me using dreams as a substitute for story.

If I've missed anybody, I'm sorry. Rest assured there'll be another book!

Simon Paul Woodward
London. December 2013.

18347492R00174

Printed in Great Britain
by Amazon